The Pirate's Booty

Inventor-in-Training,

Book One

D.M. Darroch

Illustrations by Jennifer L. Hotes

For Lily —
Embrace your
inner inventor!

SLEEPY CAT PRESS

This is a work of fiction. Names, characters, places, and incidents either are the product of the author's imagination or are used fictitiously. Any resemblance to actual persons, living or dead, events, or locales is entirely coincidental.

ISBN: 1-890797-06-5
ISBN-13: 978-1-890797-06-5

To Aidan, for laughing in all the right places

Contents

1

Angus Sets Sail

The day Angus Clark vanished began just like any other mundane school day.

By seven AM his mom had yelled at him five times to get out of bed. At quarter after seven, she reminded him for the third time to stop reading the dishwasher installation guide long enough to put on his socks. At seven thirty, she grabbed his airplane encyclopedia out of his hand and threatened to donate it to the library if he didn't finish his breakfast before the bus arrived. After some world record speed hair-combing, haphazard tooth-brushing, and a few harsh words on both sides, Angus emerged from his house just in time to scrabble on to the bus and land in the front seat as Mr. Nelson kicked the shuttle into first gear.

He didn't see his mom again until twenty minutes to ten when she delivered his forgotten lunch and gym clothes.

School wasted Angus' precious thinking time. It seemed that his teachers spent too much time on quite trivial information, like multiplication tables and grammar rules, and not nearly enough, or any time really, on the truly fascinating applications of household electronics and aviation technology.

This morning was a perfect example. His math teacher, Ms. Evergood, was going on and on about area and perimeter. That is, it was crucial to say "square" after the number when you were figuring out how many acres of grass a cow can eat, but not when you were measuring how much wood to buy to fence in that cow.

It would have been much more interesting for everyone if they could have designed the best remote control device to drive the cow. Or even just a cell phone app connected to a microchip implanted in the cow's neck, like they do at the vet's office. And after that, they could talk about alternative uses for the cow, like using it in place of ride-on mowers at city parks to reduce emissions.

So he began to think about other ways to employ this technology. Like, should he be purely capitalistic about it and rent out his cow to the neighbors on weekends? What would be a good price to cover future research and development efforts while still being a good value for weary dads who just wanted to nap on their Saturday afternoons? And of course, that led to considering other animals as well. Angus made a list. It looked like this:

ANIMALS I CAN CONTROL REMOTELY AND MAKE $$$$
1. Monkeys to save firefighters all that time climbing up and down trees rescuing cats.
2. Dogs to mop kitchen floors after birthday parties.
3. Peacocks to fan sweaty people on the beach.
4. Boa constrictors to perform the Heimlich Maneuver.

"Angus!"

Oops. By the expression on Ms. Evergood's face, that hadn't been the first time she'd called his name.

"Perhaps you could tell us the answer to number three?" she demanded.

He scanned his textbook quickly. He wasn't even on the page with the questions. He fumbled through his book, anxiously looking for number three.

"Anyone want to tell Angus what page we're on?" Ms. Evergood was using her "I'm rapidly losing my patience" voice.

"Eighty-seven," piped up Ivy. Figures. Ivy always knew what page they were on. She practically always knew the answers before Ms. Evergood even asked the question. Ivy. Such a goody-goody.

Angus found the question, rapidly scanned the word problem, quickly figured the double-digit multiplication in his head, and confidently announced, "Three hundred and sixty feet!"

"Ivy, would you please tell the class the correct answer?" asked Ms. Evergood.

Ivy smiled sadly at Angus. "Three hundred and sixty SQUARE feet."

Figures. Just another day in math class.

The rest of the school day was fairly uneventful. Except for a quick trip to visit the principal, it had been just like any other day.

He hadn't gotten into that much trouble once he had explained that he needed to balance five chairs on top of each other during social studies to illustrate an airport radio control tower. The final addition of the classroom hamsters in their cage, complete with the running wheel, had probably been ill-advised. But it wasn't his fault that Billy Roberts had chosen that moment to trip and land on the structure. Besides, it had only taken the class fifteen minutes to find two of the hamsters, and the janitor wouldn't have to remove too much of the baseboard to get the third one out of the wall.

Now he was staring out the bus window, heading home, and eager to get back into his laboratory and continue working on his newest invention.

You see, Angus Clark was way more than just an average kid. Angus Clark was an inventor in training. He had a business card to prove it.

Angus Clark
Inventor in Training
"No problem too big or too small."

Electronics * Potions * Contraptions
(Laboratory in Clark garage.)

He scratched his head thoughtfully, causing his light brown hair to stick straight up. His mom was forever making him use new hair gels and styling creams, trying to make his three cowlicks lay flat. Every day, the same thing. "Wash your face. Comb your hair. Don't forget to brush your teeth. Pick up your shoes. Make your bed." Didn't she realize what a waste of time all that was? His face was just going to get dirty again, and he'd be putting his shoes on again tomorrow.

Seriously. One day soon he'd be a famous inventor and he'd never have to comb his hair again. He'd build a robot to do it.

Angus knew he wasn't a full-fledged inventor yet. He had a lot of great ideas, but none of them actually worked.

There was the Spankmatic 3000 that he had designed when his bratty four-year old cousin visited for a week. His mom had found his specifications and had stripped Angus of his lab privileges for a month. Worse, she'd forced him to read talking train books to the little creep for the remainder of the visit.

And then there was the Olfactory Biohazard he'd developed to protect his tree house from squirrels. Okay, so squirrels don't sound that fierce. What you need to know is that before Angus had a full-fledged lab in his parents' garage, he had to store some of his machine parts in his tree house. There is nothing more frustrating than looking for a ¼-inch screw that you know you had yesterday and finding nothing but a pile of hazelnut shells. His mom didn't believe him, but he had seen light reflecting off of metal twelve feet up in the cedar tree.

Back to the Olfactory Biohazard. Angus had researched squirrels, and had learned that they were repelled by the scent of mint. He figured they were probably put off by lots of other smells, too. The more stinks, the better, he thought. So he concocted a potion of mint, raw eggs, jalapeño peppers, cold coffee out of his dad's mug, old boot water, several of his mom's baking extracts, laundry detergent, cat litter, and the best ingredient of them all, fish emulsion from the garden shed. He mixed them in a bucket, and left it in his tree house to develop a potent aroma.

It was coming along pretty nicely, a thick green film growing across the top, when he decided it was time to transfer it to a spray bottle. He was carrying it down the ladder from his tree house when his boot got stuck in a rung, and the whole glorious disgusting rancid mess cascaded down on top of him.

His mom had to wash his clothing three times to get the stench out, and he was just now able to eat finger foods without gagging. The more he thought about it, that invention would have functioned marvelously. Maybe he'd give it a second try.

But none of his designs had failed as miserably as the Anti-Meow Tongue Spray.

The concept was solid. His mother's fat orange cat Sir Schnortle waddled around all night howling piteously to be let outside. She was afraid he'd be eaten by raccoons, so Angus and his dad had to endure the beast's deep-throated mewls. Just when Angus had finally fallen to sleep, the two-ton feline would climb on to his chest, nearly smothering him, and announce "MEEOOOW" at the top of his cat lungs.

Clearly, something had to be done.

Angus borrowed some library books about herbal remedies. It wasn't his preferred reading material, but desperate times called for desperate measures. His idea was solid, and his research was thorough. The Anti-Meow Tongue Spray should have worked. It may have been a calculation error; his lemon mint to bergamot ratio was slightly skewed. However, it could also have been a geometric mistake; his angle of aim was a bit off. Whatever the cause, he had the scar to prove that cats don't appreciate being nailed squarely in the left nostril by herb spray.

Angus banged open the front door, shrugged off his backpack, and dropped it to the floor with a thump. He raced through the hallway to the kitchen where his mother was peeling carrots for dinner.

"How was school today?" she asked, without looking up from the sink.

"Hmmph," responded Angus.

"That's nice, Dear. Put away your shoes wash your hands hang up your coat," she replied.

Angus grabbed a bag of snack crackers from the cupboard and headed for the garage. Air from an open window in the kitchen grabbed the door and slammed it shut behind him.

He could barely hear his mom yell "Angus!" through the thick wood door.

He strapped on his mustard yellow tool belt, adjusted his plastic safety glasses, and was sure to check that his screwdriver was in its place. A screwdriver was the most essential tool an inventor could own.

Angus gazed lovingly around his laboratory. To the untrained eye, Angus' cabinet of scientific wonders looked much like an old work table piled high with broken kitchen appliances, screws, nuts, bolts, tin cans, milk cartons, and tattered magazines with a few computer innards and light bulbs thrown into the mix. On the floor, a collection of plastic bins of various sizes and colors contained rocks, slabs of wood, old PVC pipe, wires, and an array of electronic components.

To Angus, this table represented all the possibilities in the universe. In the upper left corner were the components he had sorted last week to build a robotic gum chewer: his mom's broken bread machine, red and green colored wires, a mini-light bulb from his dad's old flashlight key ring, and an empty wrapper of bubble gum. He'd chewed the bubble gum while redrawing his blueprint, so he'd need to buy some more before building the robot.

On the floor to the right was a drawing of Sir Schnortle. The consequences of his Spankmatic 3000 failure had taught him not to leave around specifications that just anyone, especially his mom, could read. To those less scientific than he, the picture looked like an upside-down box with wheels. Only he knew that suspended from either side of the box was a bungee cord hammock. Harnessed into the hammock was a full-body leotard perfectly sized for a cat of profound girth, and sound-cancelling head gear with cat ear holes. He had gotten the idea while watching wrestling with his grandfather one weekend. He was considering calling this invention the Cat Muffler.

Directly in front of him was his current work-in-progress. He was more excited about this invention than any he had designed before. Yesterday, it had actually started to make a humming noise! This particular invention, the Insect Incinerator, was built from a handheld barcode scanner.

His father often brought home defunct electronics for Angus to disassemble. His mother complained about all the "clutter in the garage", but invention is a messy business. This time, Angus had thought he'd just try to get the scanner to work again, but then he thought it would be a better idea to improve upon the original design and roast some beetles in the process.

He picked up the Incinerator, flipped the "on" switch, and on a whim, pointed it at a pile of cedar cones resting on top of his rock bin, and pulled the trigger. The scanner vibrated and grew warm in his hand, and then there was only smoke where once there were cones.

Angus stood as if struck by lightning, mouth agape, then closed and reopened his eyes. He smacked himself in the head, and looked again. Sure enough, the cones had vanished. He turned and ran to the backyard. Beneath the cedar tree lay piles of cones and needles. Angus aimed the Incinerator and pulled the trigger. Again and again, the machine hummed, grew warm, and smoke replaced the cones.

"It works! It works!" Angus yelled, jumping up and down and running in frenzied circles like a dog just released from the kennel it's been confined to all day.

"Yahoo!" He yelled, throwing his hands in the air, accidentally releasing the scanner to sail through the air. Angus' stomach lurched as he heard his Insect Incinerator smack a large boulder. He ran to where the scanner had landed, hastily retrieved it, pointed it at a cone, and frantically squeezed the trigger. Nothing. Again and again he tried, but there was no humming, no vibration, no warmth, and absolutely no smoke.

Angus kicked the boulder, instantly regretting it as he remembered he was wearing flip-flops, not shoes. He limped back to his lab, grabbed his trusty screwdriver and began to open the back of the scanner. Yesterday, after he had crossed red and blue wires with a green one, the Insect Incinerator began humming. Maybe if he added a yellow one he could repair the damage caused when the machine bounced off the boulder.

"Angus!"

His mom's voice directly behind his right ear startled Angus, and his screwdriver clattered to the floor.

"Yes, Mom?" he asked.

"This garage is a mess. I need you to get some of this trash off the floor so your dad can fit the car in here."

"But Mom, I'm in the middle of something," whined Angus.

She spoke in a voice that brooked no argument. "Do it. Now. And add some water to this baking soda to wipe down the table." A puff of powder escaped the lid as she plunked the orange box on his work table.

"It's not trash," Angus mumbled to his mom's exiting backside.

Angus gave a deep sigh and looked longingly at the partially opened Insect Incinerator. He bent over to pick up the screwdriver, and thumped his head on the table, biting his tongue and spilling the baking soda out of the box and into the exposed electronics of his invention.

"Ouch!" he cried, gingerly touching the inside of his mouth. He looked at his wet finger and noticed a bit of blood from his tongue. Great. This afternoon was just getting better and better! He'd better move his invention out of the way before anything else happened to it.

Without wiping the saliva from his hand, he reached for the Insect Incinerator. As his damp fingers grazed the exposed circuitry, he felt a burning sensation and smelled smoke. His head spun dizzily, enough to turn his stomach. In the depths of his nausea, he realized he could no longer see. It became utterly quiet. Then, there was nothing.

Gradually, he came to his senses. He heard seagulls screaming and water rushing. His tongue throbbed. Something prickly was poking into his back.

The first thing he noticed when his vision returned was that he was sitting on a mound of cedar cones and needles.

The second thing he saw was the group of pirates leering at him.

2

Angus "Joins" the Crew

Angus squeezed his eyes shut and smacked himself in the head.

"Wake up wake up wake up," he chanted.

He opened his eyes again. Five pirates were still staring at him. Five filthy, stinky, crazy-looking pirates. And one parrot.

"Blimey lad! Are ye squiffy? Get off yer bum, clean up that mess, and swab the deck!" shouted a burly female pirate, who despite tangled dreadlocks, missing and yellowed teeth, and a scar on her forehead, bore an uncanny resemblance to his math teacher, Ms. Evergood.

Angus rose unsteadily to his feet and caught the mop thrown at him by a short, stocky male pirate dressed in a torn red shirt and ragged blue trousers. He felt a splinter pierce his index finger. This was the most realistic dream Angus had ever had. He could smell Red Shirt's unwashed clothing. He could feel his fair skin burning in the bright sunlight and the cool wind drying the sweat from his hair. The ground rocked beneath his feet.

"What's that on yer face?" asked Red Shirt.

"What? Where?" said Angus, fumbling around to touch the safety goggles still fastened snugly around his head.

The big female pirate swaggered across the deck.

"Hand 'em over," she demanded.

"They're just my goggles," said Angus.

"Now," she growled.

Angus pulled them off his head, and quickly placed them in Ms. Evergood's outstretched hand. She held them up to the sunlight, turned them over, looked through them, and flung them at him.

"Worthless," she pronounced. "But I will have that yeller belt ye're wearin'."

Angus unbuckled his tool belt, let out a deep sigh, and gave it to the pirate.

"And yon sparkly thing will be a nice addition to the coffer." She pointed to the Insect Incinerator resting on top of the cone pile. She snatched it up quickly before Angus could protest, and marched off to the front of the ship.

"If I catch ye hornswagglin' the crew again, ye'll walk the plank," she yelled back.

"Better get to swabbin'. Marge is in a murderin' mood today," muttered Red Shirt.

Angus wobbled around the rocking deck and began swiping the mop to and fro, pushing the cedar cones from one side of the ship's deck to the other. He saw light gleam from beneath the needles. On closer inspection, it seemed his screwdriver had been buried at the bottom. He must have dropped it when he fell onto the pile. He glanced around furtively. None of the pirates was watching him. He reached down and retrieved the screwdriver, sliding it into his pants.

"This is some crazy dream," mumbled Angus.

"It's not a dream," replied the parrot.

Angus stopped moving cones around and examined the bird. The yellow-breasted fowl clung to some low riggings. It stretched out its florescent blue wings and flapped slowly, swinging itself upside down. Small, intelligent eyes scrutinized him from a slightly cocked head.

"Pretty bird," sang Angus, reaching out to touch its soft stomach.

"Hands off!" croaked the parrot, biting Angus' outstretched finger.

"Ouch! Stupid parrot!" shouted Angus, sucking on his injured digit.

"Who are you calling stupid? And technically, I'm an Ara ararauna."

Angus stared wide-eyed at the talking bird.

"Scientific term for blue-and-yellow macaw," finished the parrot.

Angus gaped.

"Why are you acting so weird, BP?" asked the bird.

Angus took a closer look at the bird. Parrots were mimics, he knew, repeating words they'd heard people say over and over again. But this animal was different. It almost seemed as though it was having a conversation with him. This was a strange dream.

The bird cocked its head to the left and regarded him. It cocked its head to the right, half squinting its eyes. Then it jumped back, fluttered into the air as though startled, and flew just out of reach. It glared distrustfully at Angus.

"Who are you and what have you done with BP?" demanded the bird.

"Are you actually talking to me?" responded Angus.

"No one else here but you, me, and the mast," retorted the macaw.

"Can you actually understand what I'm saying?" Angus pinched himself, hard. When that didn't wake him up, he slapped himself across the cheek. "Ouch!"

"Who are you, and what is wrong with you?" asked the astonished bird.

"Why can't I wake up?" Angus slammed the pointy end of the mop into his kneecap. "Ow!"

The macaw grimaced. "Please stop maiming yourself! I can't watch it anymore." The bird hopped off its perch and glided closer to Angus, landing on his shoulder. Angus could feel its warm breath in his ear. "No, you're definitely not BP. You look like him, but you don't have any piercings in your ear. BP has two holes on the left side, and one on the right." The bird flew back to the rigging.

"So the question remains, what have you done with BP?"

Angus answered, "I don't know anyone named BP. My name is Angus Clark, and I'm an inventor in training. I have no idea how I wound up in this dream, since I haven't been interested in pirates since I was six. Why would my subconscious have created this dream? The last thing I remember was being in my lab, trying to fix my Insect Incinerator, then I fell asleep or fainted, and now this. Wow, do I feel sick. How do I get myself to wake up?"

"Whoa," said the macaw. "Angus? Angus Clark! That means you did it! You actually did it! I was so hoping you'd figure it out! Do you know what this means? I can go back! You can help me get back!" The macaw leaped enthusiastically from its perch and flew in rapid circles around Angus' head, cheering as it went. After several turns, it settled on Angus' shoulder.

"So what did you use? A potion, a wormhole generator? How do we get back?" The macaw peered at Angus.

Angus stared blankly back.

"Wait a second ... do you even know what you've done?" asked the macaw. "Do you know where you are?"

"On a pirate ship in the middle of the weirdest dream I've ever had. Maybe I'm getting the flu. I always have weird dreams when I'm getting the flu. I wonder if I'll even remember this when I wake up," said Angus.

"But Angus, that's just it. You won't remember it when you wake up. You're not going to wake up. You're already wide awake. This is really happening," insisted the bird. "You still don't get it. Stick out your finger."

Angus complied, pointing his index finger to the sky. In a blur, the macaw clamped down on the finger with its beak, biting as hard as it could.

"Ow! Get off! Let go, you rabid bird!" Angus shook the bird free. He glanced down and watched red droplets well up from his injured finger. He popped it into his mouth and tasted the salty, metallic blood. "What did you do that for?" he lisped, his tongue tripping over his finger.

"Have you ever bled in any of your dreams? Did you ever feel pain like that and not wake up?" asked the macaw.

Angus realized he'd never had a dream this vivid. All five of his senses were awake and alert. He gagged and pulled his finger out of his mouth. If he wasn't dreaming, what did that mean? What was happening here?

The macaw read the confusion and fear in his eyes. "Sit down—over there, on that cask."

Angus dazedly settled on a wooden whiskey barrel, the metal rim digging into the backs of his thighs. He was still holding the mop.

"Okay, comfortable?" asked the macaw. Angus could have sworn there was concern in its eyes.

"So tell me again, in detail, what were you doing right before you got here?"

Once again, Angus related his tale. This time, he explained the problems he'd been having with the Insect Incinerator and how he had planned to modify it. The macaw listened intently, now and again nodding its head and making murmuring noises. More than once it whistled and said, "Brilliant!" When Angus had finished his account, the bird asked, "And this Insect Incinerator ... you're certain it was incinerating the cedar cones, and not, perhaps, merely transporting them elsewhere?" The bird flapped its wing pointedly in the direction of the piles Angus had been making.

Angus looked at the cones and needles and an idea began forming in the back of his mind, a realization so frightening and wonderful, it made him shudder. "Do you mean," he began, "I've incinerated myself? Only, the Incinerator I built doesn't actually burn things, but just, moves them ... moves them ... where?"

Angus thought back on everything he'd learned in school and read in newspapers and magazines. He knew that piracy today mainly involved the theft of digital music and computer software. And except for during Halloween, nobody wore three-corner hats and patches over their eyes. The crazies on this ship were wielding swords and daggers. There was a cannon in the front of the ship. Did anyone even use cannons anymore?

Angus felt dizzy and nauseous. Oh no, was he going to black out again?

"Put your head between your legs. Breathe in. Deep breaths, Angus. Slow and steady. You'll get your sea legs soon." The macaw flapped its wings, fanning Angus.

"I'm okay. Just tell me. Where am I?" asked Angus.

"Sail ho!" yelled someone from atop the rigging.

The macaw hopped off Angus' shoulder and flew over his head. "Quick, get back to mopping. We'll talk later." It flapped off, and Angus turned around queasily. Marge was marching toward him with purpose. Angus stumbled to his feet and began pushing the mop back and forth mechanically.

"Leave off that, ye bilge rat, and fetch me the spyglass," she ordered, thrusting a set of keys at him.

Angus rested the mop against the cask and took the keys, unsure what to do with them.

"In the captain's quarters!" she yelled at him.

He turned in a circle, wondering which way to go. "Ye scurvy dog! Aft! To stern! What ails ye today?!"

He turned toward the rear of the ship and glimpsed a high deck. Just beneath was a small room. He tripped to what he assumed was the captain's cabin and worked through each key until he found one that opened the locked door. A primitive telescope rested on a heavy worm-eaten desk. It slid precariously from one end of the desktop to the other. Angus grabbed it and bumped into the doorway as the boat rocked sideways. He wobbled back to Marge as quickly as he could, feeling as though he'd just climbed off the scrambler at the state fair. He thrust the telescope into her outstretched hand, then promptly bent over and vomited all over her boots.

Without warning, Marge struck him across the ear with her large, grimy hand. He yelped in surprise and pain, and heard the blood rushing in his ears.

"Ye're a poor excuse fer a pirate, ain't ye? Outta me sight!" barked Marge. She clamped the spyglass to her eye and chortled. "Blimey! She's a big one, she is! Let's bring a spring upon her cable and load the chase guns with case shot!"

She was speaking English, but Angus had no idea what she was saying.

"Shove those cases into the cannon at the bow and then wait," yelled Red Shirt as he ran past. "And hold on, we're comin' about."

Angus grabbed the side of the ship as it began to turn violently into the wind. Just in time, too; the angle and speed of the ship would have flung him overboard if he didn't have a handhold. He had a sneaking suspicion that if he had fallen into the sea, the pirates wouldn't have come to his aid. He silently thanked Red Shirt, smelly or no.

Once he regained his footing, he set off to the front of the ship. Empty cans stuffed full of rocks, bits of wood shards, and other hard and sharp detritus rested in boxes along the side of the cannon. Apparently, he was meant to load the cannon with these cans. They were deceptively heavy, and he struggled to lift one after another into the mouth of the cannon.

A wave crashed over the side drenching him and the boxes with bone-chilling seawater. He shivered in the wind, and shook his head to clear the water from his ear. It still ached from Marge cuffing him, but the nausea seemed to have passed, for now.

"Stand ready, matey! We'll run a shot across her bow," chortled a scrappy young pirate sporting an eye patch. His curly blond hair was cut close to his head, and his brown eye sparkled. He looked remarkably like Angus' mischievous friend Billy Roberts, especially as he bounced exuberantly from one foot to the other. Billy never could sit still.

Angus gripped the ship's rail and gazed into the distance. He glimpsed a two-masted ship in the distance, and was astonished to discover how rapidly they were gaining ground.

"Are we chasing them?" he asked Billy.

Billy stopped moving briefly, and looked sideways at Angus, brows wrinkled in bewilderment. "Are we chasing them?!" His face cleared, and a slow grin stretched across his face. His brown eyes twinkled deviously. "Arrr! Ye almost had me there, bucko! Shep'll have us there right quick. I'm not too sure about this first shot, though. Untested ammo. Be ready to jump out of the way soon as we light her. Might be some recoil."

"You mean, we're going to shoot the other ship?" Angus gasped. "But, we could hurt someone! What if it sinks?"

"Har-har-har! Ye are a funny scallywag, BP! Most we'll do is destroy her mast and rigging. Won't sink her til after. No prey, no pay, savvy. Should be some good plunder in the hold. Got yer dagger ready in case we board? Ye've got to show Marge ye're more than a powder monkey if ye ever want a cut of the booty. She's on ye today though, ain't she?"

Angus' mind reeled. He'd incinerated himself on to a pirate ship that was about to attack another ship, potentially causing large scale damage and loss of life. Worse, he had personally loaded the cannon that would enable this robbery on the high seas. His math teacher, normally a very strict and respectable member of the community, was a toothless pirate who smelled of bacon and wore men's boots. His school friend, who, if truth be told, did often spend time in the principal's office, had now completely devolved into a one-eyed explosive-crazed maniac. All Angus wanted right now was to find that macaw and get an explanation for all this insanity.

As if it had read his mind, the bird fluttered down to his shoulder and spoke quietly so Billy couldn't hear. "Just go with it. I'll explain everything after the battle. We have to get you off this ship. In the meantime, you need to keep your wits about you. Do you have a weapon?"

Angus shook his head no.

"You need something sharp. Pointy. BP always has a dagger with him. Can you find something?"

Angus felt the waistband of his pants. "I've got a screwdriver."

"That will have to do. Be alert once the shooting starts. Stay out of the way of the cannon or it will crush you. And whatever you do, keep clear of Marge."

"Fire in the hole!" yelled Billy.

"Run!" squawked the bird.

3

The Plank

Angus ran as far from the cannon as he could, and was hurled to the deck as it exploded. The blast was deafening. Wood shards and rocks hailed down around him. Angus' head throbbed from the noise and the acrid gunpowder stung his eyes and throat. He coughed violently and looked back through teary eyes at the hole the cannon had blown through the side of the ship. Not the side of the merchant ship. The side of the pirate ship. Flames ate into the decking where it met the rails.

"Arrrrrrrrrrrrr!" Marge was shrieking at a decibel level that could deafen a bulldog. "Where is that good-fer-nothin' bilge-eatin' swill-drinkin' scurvy dog? Get me that bilge rat's head in a noose! I'll carve him up meself! He'll be walkin' the plank and no mistake!"

"Quick! Run round the other side! She's goin' to kill ye this time fer sure!" gasped Billy, lying beside him.

"Me? What did I do?"

"Overloaded the cannon with bad shot. Too heavy. Couldn't aim. Ye're done fer, mate. Off to Davy Jones' locker if Marge catches ye. Hide!" breathed Billy before he fainted.

Angus lumbered to his feet and lurched to the side of the ship. Smoke blanketed the air, giving the impression of thick fog on deck. He slipped in water lapping against his ankles. He bent down, removed his flip-flops, and padded stealthily to the ship's stern. Where was he going to hide on this vessel? Marge would find him eventually, and then what would happen? He couldn't avoid her forever. He peered over the side of the ship. Jumping made no sense. There was no land in sight, none that he could see through the smoke anyway. He'd probably drown before he ever reached shore. Besides, he still hadn't found out where he was, how exactly he'd arrived here, and how he could get home.

"Squawk! Below decks!"

The macaw zipped past his ear. Angus tottered along behind the bird as rapidly as possible given the listing of the ship. He heard the disembodied voices of men shouting to each other from among the riggings. Close by, Marge barked orders and cursed

Angus' existence. He couldn't see two feet in front of his face, and he hoped he wouldn't trip over her while trying to avoid her.

The bird landed on a metal ring attached to the deck. It squawked at Angus, and he reached down and pulled at it. The deck opened, revealing a ladder built into the hull. The bird flew ahead of him down into the belly of the ship. Angus stuck the flip flops in his pockets, gripped the ladder rungs tightly, and headed below deck, careful to close the trapdoor behind him.

Five slippery rungs, and he was standing inside the ship. The air was dank, reeking of unwashed bodies, damp clothing, and moldy bedding. Dim lanterns glowed along one wall.

"Yuck! I hate it down here! Pirates are such filthy creatures!" complained the macaw.

"What do you suggest I do now?" asked Angus, slipping on his flip-flops. His mom had always told him not to shower barefoot in the school locker room, and looking down at the floor of the pirates' bunkroom, he now understood her reasoning.

"I haven't figured that out yet. Getting you off the ship is going to be easier than I had originally thought. If Marge finds you, she'll toss you overboard herself. But that wasn't exactly the method I had in mind," said the macaw.

Angus covered his face with his hands and sighed. What a disaster this day had become! He now fully believed that this was no dream. He was on a burning pirate ship that was dangerously close to sinking. If he survived that, a murderous giantess was keen to drown him.

"Even though you're a parrot, sorry, macaw, you seem to be the only one on this doomed ship I can understand. Before this day gets any worse and I wake up dead, would you please tell me where we are, and how you think I got here?" asked Angus.

The macaw considered the closed trapdoor. "Everyone's topside struggling to put out the fire and get the ship back under control. I can give you the three second version, but then we've really got to develop a plan of action."

The bird began. "You're on a sloop named The Fearsome Flea. A sloop is a single-masted ship known for its speed and shallow draft. It can get in and out of tight spaces and shallow waters, and is easy to maneuver. Maniacal Marge is the tyrant running this ship. The other crew members are terrified of her."

"Okay. I'm on a ship with a crew of crazy people. That much was obvious. But where are we? Geographic location, I mean. And why are these people dressed like pirates?" asked Angus.

The bird took a deep breath. "Because they are pirates. And you're in the Puget Sound, near Seattle."

Angus wrinkled his brow in consternation. Seattle was only twenty miles from his house. Surely, he would have heard something on the news about pirates sailing the local shores.

He shook his head. "No, that can't be. There are no pirates in Seattle, the state of Washington. No pirates in the entire continental US. Haven't been for ..." Angus tried to remember his history lessons. "Two hundred years!"

The macaw regarded him sadly. "That's true, Angus .... in your world. In this world, pirates roam freely over all the American waters. Be glad you didn't end up on Lake Erie. The Great Lakes pirates are notorious."

"My world?" questioned Angus. Now he was more confused than ever. His head began to spin again, but this dizziness had nothing to do with the ship's movement.

"Of course," said the macaw. "You really don't get it, do you?" Angus' empty stare was answer enough. "You've transported yourself, apparently accidentally. You understand that bit, right?"

Angus nodded.

"You haven't just moved your body to another place on the earth. You transported yourself to a parallel universe," said the bird.

Angus stared blankly.

"You have no idea what I'm talking about. This gets better and better." The macaw was exasperated. "He solves one of the greatest scientific mysteries of all time and doesn't even realize it. Typical."

The macaw stopped talking for a moment, glanced up at the closed trapdoor, and said, "Sounds like they're still at it. We've got a bit of time. You'd better sit down."

Angus collapsed on to the nearest bunk, releasing a puff of dust and dirt from the scratchy wool blanket.

"In your world, your universe, are there pirates?" asked the bird.

"Not anymore, except for a few places in Africa. And they don't sail ships like this or dress like this. Pirates like this haven't existed for hundreds of years," answered Angus.

"Exactly. So logically, you agree this is not your world?" asked the bird.

"Well, unless we're in a movie or at an amusement park ..." mumbled Angus.

Feet stomped across the deck, and Marge's loud, angry voice vibrated through the ceiling. The bird stopped a moment, and looked at him. "Does this look like a movie or amusement park to you?"

"No," said Angus. He thought for a moment, and then asked, "So you're saying there are two worlds, or universes, and I've somehow sent myself to this one?"

"Ummm, not exactly," said the bird. "There are multiple universes. I don't know how many yet."

Angus stared distrustfully at the bird. "And just how would you know that?"

The macaw flapped to Angus' bunk and settled down beside him.

"Because I've been to several of them."

"You? How does a bird travel between universes?" asked Angus.

The bird looked sadly at Angus. "I'm not a bird. I'm Ivy."

"Ivy?!" Angus gently touched the macaw, its feathers smooth and velvety against his fingers. The bird was a bit of a know-it-all. Maybe it was Ivy. "But I just saw you at school today."

"You saw the Ivy of your universe."

"So you live in …"

"A different world than yours. Not this one."

"What are you doing here?"

"Looking for you."

"Me?"

"In my world, you're a bit of a science geek."

Angus glared at her.

"Sorry, I mean, you're really smart. We aren't the best of friends. I don't know why …"

"Because you think you know everything, and you're the teacher's favorite, and …"

"Oh, so we aren't friends in your world either?"

Angus looked at her. "Ding, ding, ding," he said sarcastically.

"Well, I need your help. Desperately. I've been moving from universe to universe, trying to find a version of you who could help me solve my problem."

"Wait a second," Angus thought for a moment. "There are multiple versions of me?"

"Well, no. Just one of you in each universe."

Angus stopped for a moment and considered this bit of news. "That's pretty neat! Am I an inventor-in-training in all the worlds?"

"In this world, you're a pirate, so no."

"Wow! That is so cool!"

"You have no idea."

"So why are you here as a macaw, and not as yourself?"

"That's the problem I was telling you about." Ivy looked like she was about to cry, if birds could shed tears.

Angus respectfully picked up Ivy and rested her on his shoulder. She rested her head against his and began her story.

"In my universe, I have a sort of laboratory in my basement. Kind of like the one you mentioned in your garage. My specialty is herbs and potions, not electronics. I generally use rats and mice to test my mixtures, but strange things have been happening with the animals. They've been disappearing, and I wanted to know where they were going. I know it was stupid, but I just had to figure it out. Not knowing was driving me crazy. Do you understand?"

Angus nodded his head.

"One afternoon, I did it. I gulped down the potion, and then it was like I was watching myself. I mean, I guess I was watching myself. I saw my body lying on the floor surrounded by the broken glass of the vial. I watched my mom find me, and yell, and cry. I saw the paramedics put me on a stretcher and take me to the hospital. I saw myself in a hospital bed hooked up to wires and machines."

"That makes no sense, Ivy. How could you see all that?"

"It made no sense to me either. Then I realized I was seeing myself from weird places, like from the ceiling, sideways from the wall, up close on top of my own nose. And the view I had of myself was like hundreds of television sets. I figured it out when I saw myself in the hospital bed from a mirror. There was a fly on the mirror, and I realized I was seeing myself out of the fly's eyes. In fact, I was the fly!"

"Ivy, that's ..."

"Crazy! I know! I was like you. I thought I was dreaming, or hit my head, or I don't know what. Then I thought if I can be a fly and still think like me, what else could I be? I saw a squirrel running across the hospital parking lot, and I imagined what it would be like to be a squirrel, and then I was in the squirrel's body. I ran underneath some parked cars for a while, but that got boring. So I tried it again with a crow. That was a lot better. I could fly and see things from high above, and I was big enough to not get swatted. I spent the rest of the day transporting my mind into different animals. Bugs too—grasshoppers were especially fun. You have no idea how wonderful it is to be able to jump twenty times the length of your own body."

"Well, if you could do that, why didn't you transport your mind back into your own body?" asked Angus.

Ivy sighed. "It was pretty fun trying out all the different animals, and it didn't occur to me until dinnertime. I started getting hungry when I was a ladybug, and I couldn't imagine eating aphids! But it wouldn't work. I looked at my body lying in that hospital bed and I focused all my energy on it, like I'd done with the animals. I focused really intently, and the next thing I knew, I was looking at myself walking around and doing things. Only, it wasn't me. It was someone in a bonnet and petticoat who looked like me. It wasn't the hospital room. It was a grassy field. It wasn't my universe. I was in the body of a spider, and the alternate Ivy was pointing at me and screaming."

Angus picked up Ivy, moved her from his shoulder to his knee, and looked at her intently. "Then what happened?"

"I focused on the alternate me, and I tried to put my mind into her body, my body, and changed universes again. It happened again and again. Every time I found another version of myself and tried to jump my mind into the body, I'd switch universes. I was so scared ..." Ivy broke off, and began gasping with her mouth open, her macaw chest pumping in and out.

Angus stroked the feathers of her head soothingly with a finger. "It's okay, Ivy. I'm here. We'll figure this out."

"At some point, I realized I needed help. I couldn't talk to the alternate versions of myself. I started to think, who could help me figure this out? In my world, you're scarily smart. But I had drifted so far away from my own universe, I wasn't sure how to get back to the you that could help me. So I decided I'd move through universes until I found a version of you that was similar to the Angus in my world."

"And did you?" asked Angus. "Can he help you, this world's version of me, what's his name, BP? Is he going to help you?"

"No, he's a buffoon," said Ivy.

"Oh."

"A dumb ape. A nincompoop. A regular knuckle-dragging cretin," added Ivy.

"Fond of him, are you?" observed Angus.

Ivy cocked her head and scrutinized Angus. "The strange thing is, one minute that creep BP was standing on deck, being pelted in the head by cones falling out of the sky. The next minute, you were lying there, looking just like him but wearing goggles and that belt. I haven't seen BP since. So I'm wondering. When you appeared, where did he go?"

They stood silently for a moment, thinking. Ivy began again. "I think you might be able to help me. You might even be smarter than my world's Angus. I mean, you figured it out. You transported yourself here—your entire body, not just your mind. You can help me get back to my universe!"

"But I don't know how I did it," said Angus. "I think it had something to do with the Insect Incinerator. I mean, that must be it, right? My Incinerator must have sent me here. But how do we make it send me back? And how can it get you back into your body? Even if we could find your world? I can't ..."

Ivy impatiently shook her head at him. "I've met mean Anguses, stupid Anguses, ridiculous Anguses, but in all the universes I've traveled to, you are the first Angus who gave up without even trying!"

Angus glared at her. "You see? That's why we aren't friends in my world. You are always so quick to judge! If you had let me finish, I was about to say I can't get started until we get my Incinerator back from Marge."

"Oh."

"I don't give up! Dumb, know-it-all, annoying ... bird!" muttered Angus.

"Sorry," apologized Ivy.

Heavy footsteps thudded above their heads and stopped at the trapdoor. Daylight flooded into the bunkroom.

"Quick! Hide!" hissed Ivy.

Angus looked around frantically, but there was no place to go. Desperate and terrified, he looked to Ivy.

"Get ready to run," she whispered.

Angus took off his flip-flops and stuck one in each pocket. He pulled his safety goggles down over his eyes and climbed quietly off the bunk. He crouched in a racer's stance, heart beating out of his chest.

"Now!" shouted Ivy as she took off, flying at breakneck speed toward the trapdoor. She flapped into the face of the tall, thin man climbing down the ladder. "Ufff!" he grunted, swatting her away. She shrieked as she bounced off the wall, and then gathered her strength and flew out the opening.

Angus shouted, "Ivy!" when he saw her crash into the hull, but then he took the opportunity her brave actions had given him. He put his head down like a bull and barreled forward, grabbing the ladder rungs and shoving the startled pirate out of his way. He was nearly to the top when he felt strong, unyielding arms encircle his waist and yank him off the ladder.

"Let go!" shouted Angus, wriggling, kicking, and flailing about. "Put me down!" he yelled, trying to bite the hands holding him tightly. His body slammed into the wall, and he fell to the filthy floor of the bunkroom. Searing pain laced through his chest as he tried to catch his breath.

A bald man with an unshaven face scowled at him. "Better say yer prayers, matey." He reached down and hauled Angus to his feet. The light entering the open trapdoor glinted off a small pistol in his hand. "Up ye go." He thrust Angus toward the ladder, and Angus pulled himself laboriously upward, gasping for air as he went.

"Got 'im," announced the taciturn pirate to the congregating crew.

Marge lumbered toward them and slapped Angus hard across the face. "Ye bloody fool! Ye nearly sank the Flea! Shep, truss him up. He'll be walkin' the plank before the hour is out."

The red-shirted pirate, whose name was apparently Shep, took Angus' arm and propelled him toward the ship's stern. "Sorry about this, lad," he said regretfully. "It was bound to happen sooner or later. Powder monkeys never last long aboard the Fearsome Flea."

Angus' mind reeled. He was in the Puget Sound, not some huge ocean. If he could stay afloat long enough, eventually he would reach shore, that is, if he didn't die of hypothermia first. The average temperature of the Puget Sound was between 40 and 50 degrees Fahrenheit. He calculated quickly in his head. A water temperature in the mid-40's would give him between 30 and 60 minutes until exhaustion or unconsciousness set in. He'd likely only survive for an hour, maybe two if he were really lucky. On the bright side, there were no major predators to worry about, at least not in his universe. He wasn't sure what creatures he would encounter in this world.

Shep stopped at the rear of the ship. For the first time, Angus noticed the six-foot-long beam jutting from the back of the ship. He had always thought "walking the plank" was a myth created by filmmakers.

"Don't run or fight, and I'll try to make this easier on ye," Shep said quietly. "Ye savvy?"

Angus nodded. Shep released Angus' arm, and picked up a pile of rope. He stretched it out between his two meaty hands, revealing a long frayed swatch. He looked meaningfully at Angus. Angus looked back, nodding his head. Shep was going to bind him with weakened rope. Shep was trying to help him! Shep wrapped the rope around Angus' body, pinning his arms to his sides. It was tight enough so as not to arouse suspicion among the other pirates, but Angus was able to move his arms slightly, and he felt a surge of optimism.

His thoughts returned to Ivy. He hoped she hadn't been too badly injured. She had flown out of the bunkroom, so he assumed her wing wasn't broken. That bald pirate had been really strong though; he had knocked the wind out of Angus' lungs, and Ivy was so much smaller than he was. He didn't see the blue and yellow macaw anywhere.

The pirates were beginning to convene around Shep and Angus. Several scrambled up the riggings for a better view. Their loud, excited voices reminded Angus of his classmates when they had an assembly, if his classmates had been stinky, hairy men with tooth decay.

"Feed them fishes, powder monkey!" yelled an aspiring comedian, eliciting a wave of laughter. "Give our greetings to Davey Jones!" shouted another. "Clean off some of them barnacles on yer way down!" sounded from the riggings. "Walk the plank! Walk the plank! Walk the plank!" chanted the crew.

In an instant, the noise quieted as Marge appeared at the ship's stern.

"Fer crimes of negligence and stupidity, and just fer gettin' on me nerves, I hereby sentence ye to death by plank. Shep, send him on his way," she ordered.

The crew roared in excitement, and began their chant once more, as Shep poked Angus gently in the ribs with his dagger. "Get on yer back and float with the current." He shoved him forward and backed away.

Angus looked down at the ice blue water racing beneath him, closed his eyes, and jumped.

4

BP Moves In

BP's eyes fluttered open. The young cannon boy raised himself up on an elbow and waited for the spinning to subside. He hadn't fainted from hunger in a while, but times were tough aboard the Fearsome Flea. He'd have to ask One-Eyed Billy if he had a food stash hidden anywhere on the ship.

One-Eyed Billy, the Fearsome Flea's gunner, was his closest ally. It hadn't taken BP long to realize that Billy's talent for finding and squirreling away foodstuffs and various other commodities made him the most popular pirate on the Flea.

Every member of the crew wanted to charm Billy. If you needed shoelaces, you might trade him a few apples. You could get matches for flea powder or saltwater taffy for a comic book. No one knew where he hid the items, but the crew spoke in muffled tones about the "extra booty" on board. Of course, Marge had no idea any of this was happening right under her nose. So far, BP had been able to elude Maniacal Marge's murderous intentions by sticking close to the well-liked Billy.

If Marge found him passed out from hunger again though, there wouldn't be much Billy could do to help him. Marge would keelhaul him for sure! He drew a deep breath, rolled to his knees, and tried to stand.

"Arghh," he moaned. He'd stood up too fast. He bent over, clutching his knees, eyes squeezed shut, and panted. The cool, hard ground rocked beneath his bare feet. He opened his eyes and gazed lazily at his dirty, brown, and callused feet. Marge, Shep, and some of the older pirates wore heavy boots. He didn't see the point of shoes. They got stuck in the riggings, tended to slip on the wet deck, squished the toes, and were a general nuisance to get on and off. They might be useful for kicking someone in the groin during battle, but so far he hadn't seen much hand-to-hand combat. Shep had given him a dirk for self-defense but wouldn't allow him to board prey vessels yet. He absently fingered the small, sharp weapon tethered to his waist with a bit of string.

He had earned his ship name with a prank that had gotten his ears boxed but had endeared him to every member but one of the Flea's crew. Maniacal Marge ruled the crew with an iron will. She had been mean and mouthy, and he had hated her from the start. She boxed his ears, screamed into his face, and stomped on his shoeless feet every chance she got. After days of her mistreatment, he had reached his breaking point.

As cannon boy, he got his food only after all the higher-ranking crew members had eaten their fill. The Fearsome Flea hadn't had decent quarry in well over a month, and rations were running low. It was finally his turn at the soup pot. No sooner had he spooned out the last drop from the empty container, but Marge barreled toward him and jostled his elbow causing him to drop his bowl and spill on to the galley floor the one meal he would have that day. She continued past him, laughing spitefully. His scarcely-contained hate for her mixed with his bedeviling hunger and exploded into white hot rage.

The howls that burst from Marge's mouth moments later were to become the source of ship shanties and crass jokes. And the small, sharp dirk that protruded from Marge's buttocks would forever label him the "Booty Poker". BP chuckled to himself remembering it.

His head had cleared and he straightened from his crouching position. His body still felt like it was moving though he stood still, the way he felt when the Fearsome Flea's crew got a few days shore leave. He realized suddenly that his feet were cold and looked down at them again. He was standing on a hard stone surface. Where was the wooden ship's deck? He looked around him and saw a table piled with strange shiny objects, shelves of cans labeled with words like "paint" and "ant spray", sandpaper, hammers and saws, and other tools. It wasn't possible. It couldn't be true. He wouldn't believe it. He was at his parents' house.

He stepped back and considered his situation, stroking his chin with his thumb and index finger like he'd seen some of the bearded pirates do. The gesture didn't help him come up with a solution to his problem, but it comforted him. His crewmates must have dumped him on shore. He was sure One-Eyed Billy was behind this trick. It was just like Billy to play jokes on the first crewman who fell asleep at night.

Once, when Shep had made that mistake, and lay face down and snoring on the galley's table, Billy had reddened his nose with a tube of cherry red lipstick. None of the pirates had told Shep and, without a mirror or washbasin on board, short, burly Shep patrolled the deck for days looking like a clown wondering why the other pirates sniggered when he told them to "keep their noses out of other people's business" and that he had a "good nose for plunder." The joke came to an end when Marge ordered him to "wash that girly paint off yer nose or I'll cut it off with me dagger."

BP would have to plan a really great trick to get his revenge on Billy for this joke.

Just then, the garage door gave a lurch, and began rising upward. A horn blared, and BP jumped out of the way, barely avoiding being run down by a metallic gray car.

"Angus! What are you doing? I almost hit you! Are you alright?"

BP was startled by the name. No one had called him that since he'd become a pirate.

"That's not me name anymore. They call me BP, the Booty Poker," he announced, folding his arms defensively across his chest.

"What's this?" asked a man, his father, chuckling. "New game, eh?" He slapped BP on the back in greeting. "Whew! Did you have gym class today? You might want to hit the shower, buddy! Now, let's see what your mom's got cooking. I'm starved!" announced his cheerful father opening the door.

"Hi, honey. How was work?" said a voice BP had not heard for years. His mother's voice came closer, "I was going to serve leftovers tonight, but the fish was fresh-caught, and ... Angus! What did you do to your clothes?" There she stood, wavy brown hair just touching her shoulders. A splash of color brightened her cheeks and lips. She pursed her lips as she peered at him, aghast. "What is that in your ears? Are you wearing EARRINGS? When did you pierce your ears?"

His eyes drank in the sight of this woman, his mother, and then he looked down at himself. What was she mad about? His jeans were ripped at the knees, ragged at the hems. His shirt had a tear through the left side where he'd accidentally ripped it with his dagger. Except for a bit of dirt and creosote, his clothes weren't even that dirty. He raised his hand to an earlobe.

"Go wash your hands right now, young man. We'll talk about your clothes and those ears after dinner," said Mrs. Clark, shaking her head.

His parents didn't seem the least bit surprised to see him. He'd run away, lived with pirates, and they were acting like they'd just seen him this morning. Had One-Eyed Billy told them ahead of time that he was coming? But when would he have done that? He didn't think Billy even knew his parents. But Billy was a sneaky, resourceful scoundrel. BP shouldn't underestimate his abilities.

BP thought about disobeying his mother. No one told a pirate what to do. Well, except for Maniacal Marge. You did what she said pretty quickly if you didn't want to swim with the fishes. He didn't have to listen to his mom anymore though, did he? But dinner did smell good, and he didn't remember when last he'd eaten.

"Angus! Didn't you hear your mother?" asked Mr. Clark.

"I was jist goin' to wash me mitts," answered Angus.

"Come on, let's wash our hands together," said Mr. Clark.

BP turned and followed him to the bathroom. Mr. Clark turned on the water and handed him a bar of flowery smelling soap.

"What were you into this afternoon, son? You really are filthy," asked Mr. Clark.

"Oh, the usual. A little pillagin' here, some plunderin' there," answered BP.

He took the sticky bar and absentmindedly rubbed it over each hand. He didn't bother to rinse, merely wiping his soapy hands on his pant leg. Mr. Clark watched him narrowly, and then followed him from the washroom.

BP marveled at the size and cleanliness of the kitchen and dining room. Living aboard the Flea and eating in its cramped, sticky galley had made him forget the spaciousness of traditional homes. He pulled out a chair and propped his elbows on the table, eager for his grub. Mrs. Clark stood at a large stove, finishing up the cooking. BP looked around the table and noticed the golden salt and pepper shakers. This booty would bring a handsome price or be a good trade for One-Eyed Billy.

He glanced furtively at Mr. Clark who was engrossed by a small black phone in his hand. Mrs. Clark's head was bent over the stove. BP's hand shot out and grabbed the salt shaker. He stuffed it into his pants, and then reached for the pepper shaker. Some floral soap still clung to his hand, and the shaker slipped from his grasp. BP fumbled with it, releasing a cloud of black powder. Oh no!

The pressure in BP's sinuses was unbearable. "AAASHEWW!" he exploded and green slime hung from his nose. He reached for the nearest thing resembling a handkerchief and wiped his face.

"Angus! You did NOT just blow your nose on my TABLECLOTH!" shrieked Mrs. Clark.

"What? Huh?" Mr. Clark's head perked up from the phone and he glared at BP from across the table.

"Go to your room! Now!" yelled the furious Mrs. Clark.

BP glared at her, and then stomped to his bedroom. This was why he'd run away in the first place.

BP hadn't always been the powder monkey on a pirate ship prowling the northern waters. His earliest memories were of walking hand-in-hand with his mother through their garden. As a young child, he had sat upon her knee learning to read as she trailed her finger along the words in a tattered book of fairy tales. His father would spend the evenings wrestling with him on the floor playing horse or building train sets.

Then he grew older, and they were always telling him what to do. He was not a little boy anymore. He had to take responsibility for himself. Good grades didn't just happen. If he lived under their roof, he'd live by their rules. His parents were always scolding him and correcting him. There were rules for everything: When he had to go to bed, how to act in school, and what type of language was appropriate. He was always in trouble with them, and they just didn't understand him.

One day, he decided he'd had enough.

Into his school bag he packed a clean pair of underwear, a jacket, a compass, a book of matches, and what was left of the money he'd received from his grandparents for his last birthday. He grabbed his sleeping bag and set off. He marched right down to the docks and joined the crew of the first ship he'd seen.

The crew became a sort of family. Billy was like a brother, alternately tormenting and defending him. Shep was the bachelor uncle trying to guide BP when he wasn't flat on his back and snoring. Marge was clearly the evil stepmother.

In the beginning, BP had missed his old way of life. Unbidden thoughts of his parents crept into his head while he was cleaning the cannons or swabbing the deck. He would force them angrily from his mind when he was awake. When he slept, dreams assailed him. Sometimes his mother was reading to him. Other times, he woke laughing from a dream of wrestling together in the grass with his father. Eventually, he had been able to corral thoughts of his parents and train himself to dream of other things, like being the pirate captain giving the order to attack.

His new life was exciting and liberating. There was always a battle to look forward to: Chasing down merchant ships, whooping at the top of his lungs while waves crashed over the ship's hull, watching and encouraging fistfights in the galley, lobbing stinkpots and cannons over the side. No one telling him to eat his vegetables, brush his teeth, or comb his hair.

And yet, as he looked around his old bedroom, strangely lived in though he hadn't been there for a while, he couldn't escape the sense of being safely at home. Now, if only he could get some grub.

5

The Swim

Any doubt left in Angus' mind about whether or not he was dreaming vanished as his body hit the frigid water. The water was so cold it felt like a vise squeezing the air from his lungs. Pain stabbed his fingers and toes. His body throbbed with each beat of his heart. He needed to breathe.

Constricted as he was by the rope kicking to the surface was impossible. He was going to sink directly to the bottom like a stone! He would die in a watery grave, and no one would know. There was no one here to help him, not a living soul. He would never see his parents again, or Sir Schnortle, or Ivy.

What would they do without him? He had just disappeared and would never return. His parents would never know what had happened to him. He imagined his mother and father overcome with grief, shriveled and gray.

He was too young to die! There were still so many problems to solve and inventions to build. His life was going to be over practically before it had even begun. He could feel panic beginning to overwhelm him.

Control yourself! You can survive this, he thought. He was a member of the school swim team for goodness sake! There was no way he was going to let his math teacher's evil twin drown him!

If he was going to survive, he would need to be rational. He closed his eyes and relaxed into the rope. He imagined tiny little bubbles of warm air pulsing through his body, and puffed up his chest as he'd been taught to do in beginner swimming lessons so many years ago. The words "belly up!" popped into his head, and his body broke the surface of the water.

He opened his eyes and drew several short breaths, careful not to inhale the salt water lapping around him. His safety goggles, not meant for swimming, were fogged and dripping. He could not see the Fearsome Flea but imagined it was long gone.

The first thing he'd have to do was to get out of this blasted rope. He'd need to cut through the frayed plies. Angus felt the rope pressing the screwdriver uncomfortably into his abdomen. His hands protruded from the rope on either side of his body making it impossible for him to reach the tool. He made small, incremental movements with his arms trying to loosen the restraints. His right arm gave way suddenly causing him to propel himself facedown into the water. He spluttered and quickly rotated himself over again. He floated quietly for a moment until he regained control of his nerves and his breathing.

The rope covered the waistband of his jeans. Angus knew he'd be unable to get the screwdriver out that way. He wriggled his fingers and felt for his front zipper. The icy water was rapidly numbing his extremities, and he had to try several times before he was able to get hold of the pull tab and slide it open. He reached in, gripped the screwdriver's handle, and slid it carefully out of his pants. If he dropped it, it would sink to the bottom of the Sound, and he'd never get out of this rope.

Forcing his anxiety back down, Angus cautiously inserted the screwdriver into a damaged ply and jabbed at it repeatedly until he felt it give way. A tiny spark of hope blazed through him. He jabbed eagerly into the next ply and the next gaining courage with each successful break. Finally, there was only one ply left. Angus could no longer feel his fingers, but he focused all his attention on keeping them gripped to the screwdriver. He pushed with his whole arm, and at last the end of the long rope was floating beside him.

He sighed with relief. Now he had to unravel himself from the cut rope. He rotated his body to the side and grabbed the rope end in his mouth. He rolled his body over in the opposite direction working one wrap off his body. He bit down lower on the rope and rolled a second time. Eventually, the remaining rope was loose enough that he could wriggle out of it.

Angus tread water and looped the rope diagonally across his chest. It was heavy and might prove a liability but he wanted to hold on to it as long as he could. An inventor in training worth the title never threw away anything useful. Then he remembered his trusty screwdriver. It was no longer in his hand. He pushed the goggles off his eyes, resting them on his forehead, and peered into the water. Nothing. His screwdriver rested on the bottom with the rocks now.

He kicked his legs powerfully, raising himself slightly in the water, and looked at the horizon. He didn't see land in any direction, and the sun was beginning to lower in the sky. He remembered what Shep had said: Float with the current. How long would it take before he reached land though? His body was beginning to shake, and he knew that he would grow colder and colder with each passing moment. He was already in the beginning stages of hypothermia. He felt the panic building again.

"Wheet wheet whoo-oo."

And now he was hearing things. He tried to remember the stages of hypothermia. Cold body, check. Shivering, check. Mental confusion, check.

"Wheet wheet whoo-oo."

He didn't think he could wait for the current to float his body to shore. At this rate, he'd be completely incoherent in another ten minutes. He needed to swim in the direction of the current; that should take him to shore, right?

"Wheet whoo-oo whizz."

A jet of water squirted him in the face. He coughed and choked trying to clear the water from his nose and throat.

"Wheet wheet, sorry, whizz."

Angus spat the water out of his mouth, blinked his eyes to clear them, and saw a huge black and white orca circling him.

"Sorry, whizz whizz. First time I've whizz been a whale whizz. Getting the hang of it whizz."

"Wha …," sputtered Angus. "A talking orca?" He tried to grab hold of his whirling thoughts. "Ivy?"

"Wheet wheet. Yup." The killer whale seemed very proud of itself. "Watch this!"

The orca dove under the water on one side of Angus and burst to the surface on his other side. It breached, lifting its entire body into the air, and crashed sideways back into the waves. Angus was swamped by a downpour of salt water. He gulped a mouthful and struggled for breath, inhaling more. He thrashed helplessly forcing his body deeper into the water. The weight of the rope around his torso pushed him down and down. The panic he had kept at bay now crashed over him, and he sank defenselessly.

Every cell in his being screamed for survival, and then he was floating, soaring, rocketing to the surface. He gasped for air and retched uncontrollably. Salt water exploded from his mouth.

He coughed, panted, and spit up more water. It occurred to him that he was no longer submerged in the water. His body was resting on a smooth, moist, firm surface. His eyelashes fluttered open. He lay straddled across a black surface. Water spritzed his forehead and cheek, and he raised his head. He was riding a black torpedo across the top of the water.

"Wheet wheet whoo-oo are you okay, Angus?" rumbled beneath him.

Angus slipped and rolled off the torpedo splashing down once more in the bone chilling water. Ivy, for it was the orca he'd been riding, swung around and gathered him up once more on her back.

"Hold on tight whizz I'll get you to land whizz," she whistled at him.

He wrapped his arms and legs around her, but it was difficult to get a secure handhold. Her large body was slick with water, and her orca muscles expanded and contracted as she swam through the water. The wind buffeting his prone body did nothing to stop the shivering that racked his bones. Angus alternated between anxiety that he would slip off Ivy again and utter exhilaration that he was riding an orca.

"Whoo-oo, Angus?" Ivy called as she came to a rest.

"Ye – es ..." His teeth were chattering so violently that it was difficult to speak.

"I can't swim any nearer whizz. Don't want to beach myself. Not been a whale before. Whizz think you can make it the rest of the way?"

Angus drowsily raised his head from where he'd rested it on top of Ivy's back. He could see the shoreline about fifty yards away, only two laps of the pool he trained in three times a week. It was the length of a practice warm up. His arms and legs shook in the cooling evening air, and he steeled himself to climb back into the water. He would just have to swim like he'd never swum before. There was much more at stake here than a mere medal.

"Maybe whizz I can get a little closer," began Ivy.

"No," breathed Angus. He rolled ungracefully off Ivy's back and plopped into the water. He was so numb he didn't even feel the water. The orca's large nose shoved him powerfully toward the beach. Off he went, kicking and stroking as hard as he could. The heavy rope weighed him down, but he knew he'd regret leaving it behind. He was nearly there. His muscles began to seize up, but he focused on the approaching beach. He must have finished one lap by now. One more to go, he thought. Kick, stroke, kick, stroke, almost there. And then his feet touched bottom and he stood.

He tripped and stumbled the rest of the way. Dry land at last! The beach was covered in rocks and boulders. Piles of cedar trees sat at the top of the tide line, their gnarled roots and trunks smoothed by the waves. The tide was coming in. Angus needed to climb up the beach away from the approaching water. Build a fire, get warm. But first, he was just going to lie down here a while and rest.

Angus dreamed of hot cocoa. He was curled up under one of his granny's afghans with the latest issue of Electronics Monthly. His dad had built a roaring fire in the fireplace. His mother was baking chocolate chip cookies in the kitchen. He smiled to himself and rolled over knocking himself awake against a large rock.

Thoughts of his current trouble washed over him, and he groaned. He opened his eyes and pushed himself up on his elbows. He was warm, wrapped in a woolen blanket in front of a blazing campfire. His sodden clothing hung from a makeshift clothesline. Oddly enough, the smell of chocolate had followed him from his dream.

"Take it easy there." A tall, spindly man walked over to him, carrying a plate of freshly baked cookies. "You had quite an adventure, I'd gather. Rest a bit and enjoy a cookie. It's my mother's recipe, God rest her soul." The man gazed beatifically into the sky.

Angus gaped in astonishment, but he was ravenous, so he eagerly grabbed a sweet, gooey cookie. He munched it and examined the man. The man stood slightly hunched over, shoulders rounded as though he were embarrassed to have reached such a great height. His black hair curled behind his ears and at the base of his neck where it had been allowed to grow, perhaps to compensate for its absence in the front. His large brown eyes were gentle and warm, like the chocolate melting in Angus' cookie. His large hands were constantly in motion, nervously running through his hair, or fiddling with a stick, or tapping against his leg.

Angus reached for another cookie. He took a delicious bite, but couldn't control his curiosity a moment longer.

"Who are you?" he asked.

The man jauntily thrust one hip out and rested a hand on it. "They call me the Howl of the Wolf," he announced confidently.

Angus bit into the cookie and looked at the man skeptically.

The man cleared his throat and tried again. "I'm known as the Vile Executioner."

Angus chewed and shook his head doubtfully.

"Some people call me Poseidon's Killer?" the man questioned.

Angus shook his head in denial and shoved the last bit of the cookie into his mouth.

"The Foul Buccaneer?"

"No," said Angus.

"Dishonor of the North?"

"No."

"Shark's Bait? Floating Cod? Jellyfish Tentacles?"

Angus crossed his arms and stared hard at the man.

The man's shoulders slumped and he kicked dejectedly at a rock on the beach. He settled down beside Angus.

"Okay, okay. My name is Hank," he said.

"That sounds about right," replied Angus.

"But I am a captain! Captain Hank," insisted Hank.

"If you're a captain, where's your ship?" asked Angus.

Hank fiddled with a clamshell. "I lost it," he mumbled.

"What's that?" asked Angus.

"It got away from me," Hank muttered.

"Once again, I can't hear you," demanded Angus.

"I lost it!" yelled Hank. "It was taken from me! My backstabbing, disloyal, faithless crew stole it!"

Angus took a third cookie and settled in for a story. He had a feeling this was going to be very entertaining.

"I am, or I was, the captain of a powerful vessel called the Fearsome Flea," Hank began. Angus' eyes bulged open. Hank noticed. "Ah, you've heard of it, I gather," said Hank.

Angus nodded. "Does my ship have something to do with your current predicament?" asked Hank.

Angus nodded again. Hank slammed his hand down angrily. He accidentally struck a rock, cringed, and grabbed his injured hand protectively with the other one.

"Marge made you walk the plank, didn't she?" Hank asked.

"Yes," said Angus.

"That would never have happened under my captainship. She has made a travesty of the entire enterprise! That's my ship! Mine!" he raged.

Angus quietly looked on.

Hank glanced at Angus and remembered himself. His anger subsided immediately and concern crossed his face. "Pardon my manners. I haven't asked about you. You didn't appear to be injured, just mildly hypothermic when I found you. Are you feeling well? Are you warm enough now? Can I get you something more substantial to eat?"

"No, no, I'm fine," Angus said quickly. What kind of pirate was Hank, anyway? Baking cookies, asking about his health?

"Good, good. And pray tell, what is your name? Or what do you like to be called?" asked Hank.

"My name's Angus. Angus Clark. I'm an inventor-in-training, and I need to get back on the Fearsome Flea."

6

Table Manners

BP heard the discussion through the bedroom's closed door. Clearly, they were arguing about him.

"I will not put up with that sort of behavior!" His mother's angry voice.

"I know, I know. The boy needs logical consequences." His father's calm voice.

"The level of disrespect! He's out of control!" His mother.

"He wasn't being disrespectful … he just doesn't think." His father.

"You are always making excuses for him! He needs to learn!" Mother.

"Yes, but something that makes sense …" Father.

"No dinner for him!" Mother.

BP gulped. The thought of going another night without a meal was more than he could bear.

"He's a growing boy. He needs to eat. I will handle this." Father.

BP sighed with relief. He would be eating tonight. He licked his lips and waited. He heard heavy footsteps on the stairs and knuckles rapped firmly on the door. He opened it and looked into Mr. Clark's stern face.

"Angus. Your mother is very upset with you, and rightly so. You know what you did was wrong, don't you?" asked Mr. Clark.

BP wasn't quite sure what all the fuss was about. Something about the table had set his mother off, but he didn't want to miss the opportunity to eat. He looked solemnly back at his father and nodded. He dropped his eyes and attempted to look contrite. He'd had a lot of practice with this act. He used it on Shep when he was about to be punished with extra chores aboard the Flea.

Mr. Clark cleared his throat. "All right then. Get down there, and be sure to apologize to your mother."

BP pushed past Mr. Clark, fearful that he might change his mind. He raced down the stairs, spun off the banister, and ran into the kitchen. Mrs. Clark stood scowling at him, her arms crossed and her toe tapping.

"I'm ... um ... I'm sorry ... Mom," BP mumbled.

"You'd better be. Right after dinner, you are going to wash the tablecloth, you hear? And we're going to talk about those ears; don't think we won't." She looked away. When she turned back to him, a small smile touched her lips. "What am I going to do with you, Angus?" She reached out, ruffled his hair, and slapped him on the behind. "Now go sit down. Let's eat before dinner gets any colder."

BP didn't need to be told twice. He hustled to the table, now unencumbered by a tablecloth, and threw himself on to his chair. Mr. Clark sat down across from him. Mrs. Clark proudly carried a serving platter piled high with fluffy rice, steaming vegetables, and juicy pink salmon and placed it gently in the middle of the table. She sat down, smiled at Mr. Clark, and began to speak, "Angus, why don't you say the prayer?"

The sight and odor of all that food was too much for the starving BP. He pulled his dirk from around his waist, and stabbed it into the salmon. He hauled a hunk of fish to his plate dropping bits of rice and vegetable on to the table. The fish slipped unceremoniously off his dirk, and he jabbed the blade into the wooden table. He broke the fish apart with his fingers and shoved it into his salivating mouth. He scooped the rice into the palms of his hands, inhaling it hastily. He picked the green bits of vegetable out of the rice and flicked them off his dish on to the table. When he'd eaten all the large pieces of fish, he picked up his dish and licked off every last morsel. His stomach was finally full. He wiped his mouth across his sleeve and belched deeply and loudly. He settled back, kicked his feet up on to the table, and began to examine his dirty toes. Only then did he glance at his parents.

Mr. Clark stared at him blankly, eyebrows raised and mouth agape. Mrs. Clark's face was bright red, and a vein pulsed in her temple. It was hard to tell what was clenched more tightly, her mouth or her fists.

He had seen that look before. It usually occurred right before Marge swatted him across the ear. He'd better move quickly. He grabbed his dirk and yanked it from the table carving out a chunk with the end of his blade. He shoved his chair back, knocking it to the floor with a thwack, and ran back up to his room. The door slammed shut on a screeching, "ANGUS!!!"

Mrs. Clark had always known that her son was a bit different. He never slept more than five hours a night, and he rarely napped, leaving her red-eyed and weary during his first year.

Young mothers are so proud to announce that their baby's first word is "Mama" or "Dada", or in the case of her niece Elsa, "Cookie". Ten-month old

Angus hadn't had a first word. Under the heading "First Words" in Angus' baby book, Mrs. Clark had written, "Close the shut off valve under the tank, remove the float arm assembly and plunger, and replace the washer. Maybe the valve seat, too."

Upon further investigation, it became apparent that the water in the bathroom adjoining Angus' bedroom continued to run every time the toilet was flushed. Baby Angus had clearly explained how to fix the problem. She made a quick trip to the hardware store, followed his instructions, and that night both she and her son slept for more than ten hours.

When Angus was three, Mr. and Mrs. Clark proudly announced to their disbelieving family over turkey and cranberries at Thanksgiving dinner that he was reading L. Frank Baum's *The Wonderful Wizard of Oz*. Granny and the elderly aunts traded eloquent looks and eye rolls with one another. Every new mother thinks her child is brilliant and special, they silently agreed among themselves.

When the pumpkin pie and coffee were served young Angus was nowhere to be found. Eventually one of the older cousins heard the hum of a hair dryer. Angus was discovered sitting cross-legged in the basement in front of the open freezer door trying to, in his words, "Generate a tornado." When pressed on the subject, he explained, "If I can only get the cool polar air of the freezer to meet the warm dry air of the blower, there should be a potential for severe weather. I think the freezer air may be too moist to form a dryline though, and I haven't figured out how to rotate my updraft."

Upon entering school for the first time in his fifth year, an increasingly independent Angus announced to his parents that from now on he would communicate only in Pig Latin. Mr. and Mrs. Clark, inclined to smile, nod, and accept his pronouncements, grew increasingly concerned after their first conference with Angus' teachers. Apparently, the other students were confused when it was Angus' turn to read aloud from Dr. Seuss. "Etha Atca Ina Etha Atha" and "Onea Ishfa Otwa Ishfa Edra Ishfa Uebla Ishfa" lost something in the translation.

Scientific experiments at the Clark house were always enlightening, often messy, and sometimes explosive. Mrs. Clark had invested in an institutional grade vacumn cleaner, five mops and buckets, and enrolled in extensive first aid training. Mr. Clark had the electrician and emergency plumber on speed dial. A few experiments had caused the garage window to be replaced three times. Mr. Clark nailed up plywood the fourth time it was broken. The lawn had been reseeded twice: Once after a flooding incident from a reclaimed water project, and the second time after an electrical short circuit of a robotized lawn edger.

Mrs. Clark fully expected destruction and mayhem so long as her son resided in the family home. Until he was on his own in the wide world, she knew her days would consist of mopping, repairing, and bandaging. She knew she had something unique and wonderful in her son, Angus, and she fulfilled her mothering duties faithfully and proudly.

However, what she would not tolerate was rude language, bad manners, and poor hygiene.

Mrs. Clark scrubbed the dinner dishes and fumed. Warm suds splashed out of the sink and dripped down the window. Perhaps she had been too tolerant of Angus. He was an eccentric child to be sure, often absentminded and distracted. He did have a streak of mischief. She suspected most boys did, but until tonight he had never acted with such utter beastliness. It was as though someone had replaced her smart, peculiar son with a naughty, ill-groomed urchin.

She rinsed the last pot in the sink and dried her hands on a towel. She wrinkled her brow and pursed her lips. Mrs. Clark was a determined woman. Once she had decided on something there was no convincing her otherwise. And right now, she was deciding that Angus needed some discipline.

Maniacal Marge herself could not have devised a crueler punishment.

BP couldn't believe his eyes. He shuddered with horror as he stared down at the fate awaiting him.

"I don't hear anything. Are you in yet?" Mrs. Clark called through the door.

"Just about," he answered. Steam rose off the hot water. It was sure to scald the skin from his body. And if that didn't kill him the bubbles would crawl up his nose and suffocate him. Walking the plank would be a kinder death.

"You still aren't in, are you?" she demanded. He pictured her sitting outside, ear wedged against the closed bathroom door.

He closed his eyes and gingerly placed a sticky toe in the water. Miraculously, it didn't melt away. He stuck in one entire stinky foot and splashed it around. He sat on the edge of the toilet and put his other foot into the bathwater. He kicked them, sure to make lots of noise. He heard the floor creak as Mrs. Clark walked away seemingly satisfied.

How long would he have to sit here, he wondered. Now that he'd satisfied his hunger, he was eager to get back to the Fearsome Flea. He wasn't certain how long this shore leave would last, and he wanted to be in his bunk before the crew raised anchor and sailed away.

When he thought sufficient time had passed, he pulled both feet from the water and regarded the bathrobe she had given him. He was puzzled by its pattern. The thick black robe was accentuated with white skulls and crossbones. How had she gotten hold of the Fearsome Flea's flag, and why had she sewn it into this ridiculous costume? And then he pictured the look on Marge's face when he showed up on deck wearing the treasured pirate flag. He grinned and wrapped himself in the soft garment.

BP unlocked the door, threw it open, and marched from the bathroom.

"Wait just a minute, young man," said a low warning voice.

He spun around. Mrs. Clark stepped from the shadows. Her sharp eyes examined him.

"You haven't bathed," she remarked coldly. "Do you know how I can tell?"

BP shook his head silently.

"Your hair is dry. Your face and hands are still filthy. And," her hand whipped out and tore the bathrobe open. "You are still fully dressed. Now go in that bathroom, take off your clothes, use soap and shampoo, and scrub! Or I will come in there with you and do it for you!"

BP gaped. Even if she was his mother, such a thing would be considered highly indecent aboard the Fearsome Flea. "How dare ye, woman! Ye shall not set foot in me bath!" he crowed.

"What?!" she cried, enraged. And then, to BP's astonishment, she snorted. As he watched, thunderstruck, air exploded from her mouth, and a high screeching noise followed. She wheezed, and sniffled, tears began running down her cheeks, and she snorted again. Egads! She was laughing!

Mr. Clark strode over to him, held his shoulder firmly, and guided him into the bathroom. "Angus, look what you've done to your mother. I haven't seen her like this since the Great Bubblegum Incident." He turned around, shut the door, and leaned against it. "Now get undressed and climb into that bath. You are about to make me angry," Mr. Clark stated calmly.

Under his watchful eye, BP peeled off his torn shirt. He unzipped his tattered pants, pulled them down to his ankles, and stepped out of them. He chastely turned his back to Mr. Clark as he removed his gray underpants. He took a deep breath and dove headfirst into the bath water.

BP spluttered and rose to the surface, bubbles covering his head like a hat. They sat on his grimy skin, tickling as they popped, and he began to giggle. The warm water caressed him, and he felt a deep happiness growing from his full stomach to the tips of his fingers. If he could, he'd purr. He closed his eyes, rested his head on the water, and then felt a hand shove him under it.

He kicked and fought and came up gasping for air. "What the?" he yelled. "Are ye tryin' to kill me?"

Mr. Clark calmly lathered up his hands with shampoo and scrubbed the top of BP's head. "Trust me, a little soap and water will not be the death of you," he said. He yanked BP's arm skyward and began scrubbing his armpit. BP's face reddened at the callousness, the inhumanity, the humiliation of it all.

"Hands off, will ye? I can do it meself," he pushed Mr. Clark away. "And ye shall not be tetchin' me bits 'n pieces."

"Fine. You won't object to me keeping you company. Just to be sure you get the job done properly," Mr. Clark said, settling down on the edge of the tub. "And you'll remove those earrings and disinfect your earlobes when you're done."

BP glared at him, lifting his lip in a snarl. Mr. Clark watched him impassively. "Looks like you could use some serious tooth brushing as well. And some dental floss."

7

Marooned

Captain Hank looked at Angus and seeing that he was serious, nodded his head.

"Okay then. I, too, would like to get back on board the Fearsome Flea. Step into my office, and we'll discuss it."

Captain Hank pushed himself up from the log he was sitting on and strode toward a ramshackle hut Angus hadn't noticed before. Angus clutched the wool blanket around his body and scrambled to his feet. He followed the captain to the structure, a lean-to made of huge driftwood logs sunk into the sand with cedar boughs for a roof. A chair was cobbled together with more driftwood and rope. A rusted slab of metal fastened to four large plastic tubs of similar size served as a table. A neatly folded bedroll rested atop a thick layer of cedar boughs raised off the sand floor by two wooden pallets. Scavenged fishing rope, buoys, rusted nails, and unlabeled cans of food lined the walls. Captain Hank motioned Angus toward the makeshift bed.

"Please, have a seat," he said.

Angus settled into the cedar boughs. The bed was surprisingly soft and fresh-smelling. Despite its crude appearance, this small abode was ten times cleaner and better organized than anything he'd seen aboard the Fearsome Flea. He looked admiringly at Captain Hank.

"Nice place," Angus said.

"Thanks. It's not much, but it's home," he replied.

"How did you get here?" asked Angus.

Captain Hank pulled a Swiss Army knife from his pocket, opened a blade, and began whittling on a piece of driftwood.

"It's not much of a story," he began. "One day I was the captain of the Fearsome Flea and the next I was marooned on this island."

"There must be more to it than that," insisted Angus.

"I was the second son of a lettuce farmer. My early years were somewhat uneventful, except for when my dog ran away from home to join the circus …"

"Maybe a little less information," interrupted Angus.

"Well, which way do you want it? First you want me to tell you more and then you say it's too much," whined the exasperated captain.

"How about you begin right before you were marooned on this island," answered Angus.

"One-Eyed Billy made me a mug of chamomile tea. I fell asleep, and I woke up on this beach," said Captain Hank.

"Okay, maybe a little farther back," said Angus.

"My early school years?"

"Too far."

"How about you ask me what you want to know," suggested the pirate.

"Fair enough," said Angus. "Why did your crew leave you on this island and steal your ship?"

"They're a bunch of unthankful, selfish, dirty, rotten scoundrels!" shouted Hank.

Angus sighed. "Did they disagree with your leadership in some way?"

Hank's hands stopped moving, and he stared incredulously at Angus. "I was a fantastic leader! One of the best on the high seas. I might even go so far as to say The Very Best! How dare you imply otherwise?"

"And yet, you find yourself marooned on this island," Angus said quietly.

The captain's mouth opened, then shut and opened again. He resembled nothing so much as a very tall, very thin, balding fish. He looked down at the wood in his hand, and began carving again.

"They may not have liked the direction our enterprise was taking," Captain Hank began. "I was only doing what I thought was right for the Fearsome Flea, for the crew, for myself. I had to follow my conscience."

Angus waited patiently for the pirate to continue.

"I've been a pirate since I was ten," said Captain Hank. "My mother traded me for a crate of sodium bicarbonate."

"Sodium bicarbonate?" questioned Angus.

"Yes! You heard me right. Sodium bicarbonate."

Angus was clearly perplexed.

The captain explained, "Sodium bicarbonate. Miracle powder. You use it for baking and cleaning or when you have acid indigestion ..."

"Yes, yes, of course I know $NaHCO3$. But what did you do to make your own mother trade you for baking soda?" said Angus.

"She was a lovely mother. The best! Do you know how valuable sodium bicarbonate is? You can't bake a decent chocolate chip cookie without it," Captain Hank said. "Not to mention how effective it is for cleaning. My mother was an exceptional homemaker." Seeing that this wasn't making an impression on Angus, he concluded, "She needed a lot of baking soda. Besides, it's not like I was the first-born son."

Angus stared at him, uncomprehending. Captain Hank shrugged and continued. "I grew up aboard pirate ships. I started off swabbing decks and cleaning galleys. I graduated to cannon boy, learned to fix riggings, and watched for merchant ships from the crow's nest. I learned all I could about sailing, and navigating, and pirating because I planned to one day run my own ship. That was made possible several years ago when I inherited some money. My dear mother, God rest her soul, perished in a grease fire."

Angus raised his eyebrows in disbelief.

"Ironic, isn't it?" said the captain. "Her beloved baking soda, instead of smothering the flames, caused the grease to splatter around the kitchen and spread the fire. My father and older brother had left town years before to escape the endless cleaning. I am the only living family member the estate lawyers could find. I inherited everything."

Angus wasn't sure if he should be sorry about the death of Captain Hank's mother or happy that the unlucky pirate had inherited money, so he settled for puzzled bewilderment.

"The Fearsome Flea was the first ship I saw. I fell in love with her immediately." Captain Hank's eyes sparkled. "I just had to have her. I paid cash, hired on a crew, and bought supplies with what was left. We had a bit of work to do to get her seaworthy but within a fortnight we were on our way."

"I ran a tight ship. The decks were scrubbed twice a day: Before breakfast and after dinner. The head was cleaned three times a day, more frequently on bean soup days or if any of the crew came down with a stomach bug. The galley sparkled; our cook observed the strictest food safety practices. I even patented my own line of cleansers, all sodium bicarbonate-based, of course," said the captain.

Angus nodded, and Captain Hank continued his narrative.

"We had a dress code aboard ship. Shirts and shoes were required in all public locations. Ripped and stained garments were repaired by our ship seamstress. The crew was required to wear ties and suit jackets at dinner," said the pirate.

"I've never heard of such things on a pirate ship," said Angus.

"Well, that was just it. Once I'd inherited my dear mother's money," Captain Hank raised his eyes skyward every time he mentioned his mother, "it became clear to me that I didn't need to fight and steal anymore to make my living. I intended to turn my life around. I began marketing my baking soda cleansers. Some major retail outlets were expressing interest in my products. We were about to set off on a sales tour. I had the crew working double time scrubbing and polishing the Flea. We were going to promote the cleansers with a spotless pirate ship."

Captain Hank reached behind some cans on the wall and unrolled a banner. It read: "Captain's Cleanser, for a Shipshape Clean Every Time." He smiled sadly.

Angus spoke. "I take it the crew didn't see things your way?"

"They were a rough lot when I first hired them on. They loved a good brawl and didn't seem to like dressing for dinner. I thought they'd come around when they saw how much money we could make legally with baking soda. I think I could have convinced them, too, if not for Marge." The captain scowled.

"Why did you hire her in the first place?" asked Angus.

"You've seen her. She's large, strong, and can keep the crew in line," Captain Hank responded. "I was busy perfecting Captain's Cleanser. I didn't have time to concern myself with the day-to-day operation of the ship. Marge had all the qualifications to be a great quartermaster. Unfortunately, it turned out she was a megalomaniac. A little bit of power made her crazy for more. She incited the crew to mutiny. If I hadn't been so caught up in my work below decks, I would have seen what she was doing above decks."

Angus said, "Seems like the immoderate love of baking soda was the undoing of both you and your mother."

Captain Hank sighed and nodded.

"Caw!"

"Ouch!" yelled Angus clutching his head. He jumped to his feet and spun around looking for whatever had just fallen through the roof and landed on his head. In his haste, he let go of the woolen blanket forgetting for a moment that he was wearing nothing beneath it.

"Caw! Yikes! Cover yourself up!"

Angus flushed crimson and snatched up the blanket wrapping it protectively around his naked body.

"Ivy, is that you?" he asked.

"Up here," she called.

Angus looked through the newly made hole in Captain Hank's roof and saw a small black crow resting in a nearby tree. Captain Hank reached down and picked up the object that had made the hole.

"My screwdriver!" Angus shouted.

Ivy, in the guise of a crow, proudly announced, "I figured you'd probably want it back."

"But how?" Angus asked. "I lost it on the bottom of the ocean! However did you find it?"

"I saw it fall out of your hand. After I left you on shore, I swam back, transported my mind into a crab, and found it on the bottom. I would have been here sooner but do you know how difficult it is to walk sideways?" she replied.

"The crow is speaking," stammered the captain.

"That's no crow. That's Ivy," said Angus taking the screwdriver from the flabbergasted pirate.

After many attempts to explain inter-dimensional travel and body jumping to Captain Hank, Angus and Ivy finally gave up. Captain Hank might be a reformed pirate, a captain of industry, and an exceptional cookie baker, but one thing was certain, he was no scientist. At last, Angus simply told him that he had trained Ivy to speak, much like the parrot on the Fearsome Flea.

Now that everyone was acquainted, it was time for Angus to put his dry clothes back on. His jeans felt like a cardboard box and his shirt was scratchy from dried salt, but Angus was happy to be rid of the woolen blanket. He slipped on his flip-flops, fastened his screwdriver securely around his neck with some frayed rope, and turned around proudly to face his friends.

"You might want to zip your fly," said a sullen Ivy, annoyed that her scientific prowess had been explained away as mere animal training.

Angus adjusted his zipper, and looked to Hank. "Well then. Let's build ourselves a boat."

"Oh, I've got a boat," said the captain.

"What are we waiting for? Let's get in!" shouted Angus.

"It won't float," said the captain. "It sinks every time."

As an inventor-in-training, Angus was well acquainted with the invention that just doesn't work. Hundreds of failed experiments had taught him to try and try again. Over the years he had learned to conquer his frustration. A defective invention meant you had to be more creative, more determined. His Incinerator was a clear example that hard work does pay off eventually, even if instead of burning up a cedar cone it conveys you to another world.

"Let's put it in the water and see what happens," he said.

The captain shrugged and picked his way over the rocks to a sheltered area. Among the sea-tossed logs rested a non-descript raft.

"That's your boat?" asked an incredulous Angus.

Captain Hank looked sheepishly at his feet. His shoulders slumped even lower than before. "I never claimed to be a shipwright," he mumbled.

Angus shook his head and whistled. "Well then, we've got some work to do. First, I need to see your recycling."

"Recycling?" asked the captain.

"Oh, right. We're on an island," remembered Angus. "I need some building materials. What have you got?"

The captain shrugged.

"Angus, the ocean's tidal field is on the other side of the island. More detritus should wash up there than on this side," Ivy chimed in.

"It's going to take some time to hike there, and it will be dark soon," said the captain.

"I can fly there and back before dark to check it out. You can hike there tomorrow if there's anything interesting," said Ivy.

"Great idea! That will give me time to draw out a plan. Now, if only I could find a pencil and paper?" Angus looked to the captain as Ivy flew off.

Captain Hank shook his head. "Sorry, nothing like that here."

Angus pulled the screwdriver off his neck and considered it. He pursed his lips and wrinkled his brow. "Got it!" he declared, and ran to the forest edge. He plunged his screwdriver into the soft bark of a cedar tree and wiggled it back and forth. He jammed his fingertips into the opening and pulled, working the screwdriver underneath the layer. He pulled and wiggled slowly and forcefully until he held a long strip of cedar bark between his fingers. He ran back to the fire.

"Can I have that?" he asked Captain Hank, pointing at the stick the captain had been whittling. Silently, the pirate handed it to him. Angus knelt down and stuck the tip of the stick into the fire until it began smoking. He pulled it out, blew on it, and put it back into the fire. After ten minutes of this, he tested it on the inner layer of cedar bark. The stick left a charcoal trail on the soft cedar bark.

"Perfect!" pronounced Angus smugly.

He began sketching, relighting the stick as necessary to maintain the dark line. Occasionally he grunted, spat on the bark, and erased an errant line with his finger. By the time Ivy had returned from the opposite beach the sun had set and Angus was rocking back and forth on his knees and looking very pleased with himself.

"I'm back!" announced Ivy.

Captain Hank hurried over to the fire from the hut where he'd been preparing a pallet for Angus to sleep on.

"Did you see any tidal booty?" the pirate asked eagerly.

"I didn't have much time to look before it got dark but there were some fishing nets and rope," Ivy began.

"Plenty of that on this beach," interrupted Captain Hank. "Anything else?"

The crow's beady black eyes glittered in the firelight. "Just a few boxes of these." She dropped a plastic object from one of her feet. Captain Hank picked up the object with his skinny fingers and held it close to the fire.

"What the?" he asked.

"Cool!" chuckled Angus, snatching it out of his hand. "I used to have one of these when I was a little kid!"

Angus held a bright yellow plastic duck. As Captain Hank watched, Angus turned the duck over and rotated a knob. He held the duck by the neck and the little plastic duck feet kicked rapidly.

"What do you do with it?" asked the interested pirate.

"It's a tub toy," said Angus. "You play with it while you're having a bath."

Captain Hank reached over and gingerly took the duck from Angus. He wound up the knob and watched as the little feet kicked. A slow smile spread over his face, and his expression was that of a gleeful child. In that moment Angus remembered the captain had spent his childhood as a slave aboard a pirate ship. He'd probably never had toys or the opportunity to play. Ivy must have been thinking the same thing because she said, "There are plenty more where that came from. Why don't you keep that one, Captain?"

The pirate looked wonderingly at Angus and at Ivy. Happiness, then distrust, and finally embarrassment crossed his face. He shoved the toy back at Angus.

"Oh, no, no. I couldn't. It's meant for children," he said gruffly.

Angus gazed at him solemnly. "I need you to examine it closely. We may need the parts for our water craft."

The captain cleared his throat. "Okay then. In that case, I'll see what I can discover." He hurried off to the hut clutching the toy.

"Well?" asked Ivy. She landed on his shoulder. "What did you do while I was away?"

Angus pointed to his cedar bark paper and showed her his drawing in the firelight.

"What do you think?" asked the proud Angus.

Ivy chose her words carefully. "Impressive. Truly brilliant. You've drawn the hull perfectly. You can almost feel the wind in the foresail."

"I know. Isn't it great?" chortled Angus.

"That rocket propulsion system is quite spectacular," she paused, then continued. "Unfortunately, there were no rockets washed up on the other side of the beach. Perhaps you might consider a small redesign?"

"What?" asked Angus. "Oh, this … no, this isn't my plan. I was just sketching the world's coolest Lego. It hasn't been built yet."

"I thought you were drawing the boat to get off this island," questioned the confused crow.

"That one is here," said Angus, picking up a smaller piece of cedar bark. Two stick figure people and a stick figure crow stood on an overturned trapezoid.

The exasperated crow flew off, cawing angrily.

"Anyone knows you're not going to find rockets washed up on a beach," muttered Angus. "Duh."

8

A Beast in the Night

Dressed in freshly laundered and pressed pajamas, BP entered the bedroom. A lava lamp suffused the room in a soft glow. The sound of waves emanated from a machine on the bedside table. The bedclothes were pulled back invitingly. BP threw himself on to the mattress. The soft feather comforter enveloped him in warmth. He nestled his freshly washed head into the two plump pillows. Warm and pink from the bath, he fell asleep immediately.

And then.

The night was quiet and peaceful. The half-moon shone down from the dark sky reflecting its cool light on the mild waves. The ship swayed gently from side to side as it progressed through the midnight waters. He swaggered jauntily toward the helm. He was the captain of this vessel. His hat, bearing one feather, sat rakishly askew. His sword rested in its scabbard, ready to be wielded. The vessel was stealthily approaching a merchant ship in the dead of night. He was cunning and sly and would catch his prey unawares. Silence reigned on deck. His crewmen waited breathlessly for his orders.

And then.

The giant hairy beast clambered upon his chest and crushed the wind from his lungs. He struggled awake bucking and kicking to escape its death grip. Was it a sea monster, or an ogre from the great beyond? "MMWROWRR!" it snarled. Eyes flashing open, he glimpsed the creature, orange and spitting, inches from his throat. With every ounce of courage he could command he struck out and seized it between his shaking hands.

He lifted it aloft bellowing in terror and fury. It reached out a razor-sharp claw and gouged at his face, shredding his cheek. He felt the fire of a welt growing and shook the shaggy, writhing brute.

"Ye may try, but ye shall not vanquish the Booty Poker!" he proclaimed with a roar.

And then.

The bedroom light blazed on scorching BP's eyes. He squinted, unable to focus on the apparition in white that stood before him.

"Angus! What are you doing? Put Sir Schortle down!" cried Mrs. Clark indignantly. She stood just inside the room, dressed in a white nightgown.

BP looked at the cat he was throttling. Ears laid flat against its head, it was hissing and scratching him. He only gripped it more tightly.

"Give him to me!" Mrs. Clark commanded. She strode to him and took the cat. "Oh now, boo boo kitty," she baby talked. "Did poor little man get scared? What did the big bad boy do to you?" She scratched the animal's ears and then placed him gently on the floor. The cat flicked its tail, threw BP a disdainful glare, and strode from the room.

"No one attacks the Booty Poker and lives to tell the tale. I'll have me due, ye black-hearted fiend!" BP yelled after him.

"That's enough, Angus. I don't know what's gotten into you today but it's late and I'm tired. We'll discuss this in the morning." Mrs. Clark turned out the light, and left the room.

BP closed and locked the bedroom door. He shoved a large bureau up against it. Even with these precautions he slept fitfully the rest of the night.

BP was relieved when the sun finally began poking through the blinds. He'd been awake for hours. He was used to rising early aboard the Fearsome Flea. It was his job to light the cook fire in the ship's galley for breakfast, even if that consisted merely of watered down coffee and stale bread crusts. After that, he had the first shift in the riggings watching for merchant and navy ships.

Landlubbers slept the morning away apparently.

He searched through the bureau drawers for something to wear. After his forced bath the night before, Mrs. Clark had confiscated his clothing wondering aloud how he'd managed to get it so dirty in such a short time. Now he couldn't believe the riches before his eyes. There must be at least five pairs of jeans here! Shirts in every color of the rainbow lay in neatly folded piles. Another drawer housed socks balled two by two, all white, not a dingy gray one in the lot. The variety was unnerving. He couldn't decide, so he closed his eyes and grabbed whatever came to hand.

Once dressed, he shoved the bureau away from the door. The lock clicked open as he turned the door's knob. He poked his head through and looked down the hallway. No sign of his arch enemy. He set off down the stairs, tiptoeing so as not to awaken the household. As he reached the last stair he heard it.

"MMWROWRR!"

BP jumped back. His hand flew to his waist but his dagger was not there. Blimey! He'd forgotten it in the bathroom last night. How was he to face the fiend with no weapon to hand?

"MMWROWRR!" the animal insisted, and then he saw it. Its eyes glowed wickedly in the shadowy gloom. It was approaching, slowly, steadily.

"Stay back, ye evil sprite! Come no closer or I shall be forced to defend meself heartily!" BP shouted.

"Oh Angus, already?" yawned Mrs. Clark, shuffling drowsily down the stairs in shabby mint green slippers. "You're up early this morning. Why not feed the cat?"

"Egads, woman! I will not give repast to an evil brute! It nearly was the death of me yester eve!" answered BP.

To his astonishment, she bent down and scooped up the creature. It closed its eyes and stretched its neck to be scratched. As she rubbed its ears, she cooed, "Good morning, my big big boy. How is my big big boy? Are you a hungry little kitty? Boo boo boo."

BP whistled. "This is worse than I thought. The dastardly creature has bewitched her mind."

BP shoveled cereal into his mouth, his eyes glued to the cat's every movement. It crunched its kibble, lapped gingerly at its water, and then began cleaning its paws. It stretched and yawned revealing its sharp teeth.

"Don't ye try to threaten me! The Booty Poker is not so easily thwarted!" crowed BP through a mouthful of cornflakes.

"Don't talk with your mouth full, dear," mumbled Mrs. Clark, head buried in her coffee cup. "Did you pack your book bag last night? Are you all ready to go?"

BP looked daggers at the cat as it strolled from the kitchen and then turned his attention to the sleepy, disheveled woman across the table.

"I'll be headin' back to the ship once I've finished me meal. I thank ye kindly fer the grub," he answered.

"Is he still talking pirate?" asked Mr. Clark. He walked to the coffee machine and poured himself a cup.

Mrs. Clark sighed. "Angus, your father and I love it that you've got such a great imagination. But you need to focus right now. The bus will be here shortly. Make sure everything is in your bag, comb your hair, and brush your teeth."

"Aye, aye, ma'am." BP saluted, stood, grabbed the bag resting beside the door, and left the room.

Mr. and Mrs. Clark stared at each other.

"That's never happened before first time I asked," said Mrs. Clark.

"Logical consequences," said Mr. Clark. "I told you it would work."

BP was eager to get back to the Fearsome Flea. The grub here was delicious, the bed warm and dry, and he might even look forward to another bath, but he could not spend another night with that fiend. How kind of his parents to arrange a bus to bring him back to the dock. That would save his feet from the long trudge.

He ran the comb through his hair once and stuck it into the bag. He picked up the toothbrush and toothpaste, considered them, and put them into the bag without brushing. He looked around the bathroom for his dagger but it wasn't there. Probably gone the way of his old clothing, confiscated by Mrs. Clark. No matter. He'd get another one soon enough. He went into his parents' bedroom, rifled through Mrs. Clark's jewelry box, and selected two gold loop earrings and two diamond studs. He dropped them into the bottom of his bag. He hurried to his bedroom, pulled the golden salt shaker from under the bed where he'd hidden it, and stashed that in the bag as well.

He ran down the stairs, and threw open the door. "Thanks fer everthin'!" he yelled as he ran down the driveway to the waiting bus.

"Angus! You're not wearing shoes!" Mrs. Clark shuffled out behind him clutching his sneakers in one hand and her coffee cup in the other.

She waved goodbye as the bus drove away. She first noticed his neglected schoolbooks beside the door an hour later.

9

At West Beach

The aroma of coffee tickled Angus' nose. He stretched luxuriantly and groaned. The incessant sound of waves reminded him that he needed to get up and empty his bladder. Eyes still shut against the morning, he leaned over to turn off his sound machine. The white noise helped him sleep through the night. He promptly rolled off on to the ground.

"Oof!" he grunted and opened his eyes. He had landed softly on the sand floor. He saw the cedar bough ceiling above his head. In his dreamless sleep, he had completely forgotten that he was no longer safely in his bedroom at home but marooned on a forested beach with a gentleman pirate and a talking crow-girl.

He got to his feet wrapping the woolen blanket tightly around his body against the morning chill and stumbled sleepily out of the hut into the foggy day. Captain Hank looked up cheerfully from the campfire where he was preparing breakfast.

"Good morning! How did you sleep?" asked the captain.

Angus yawned. "Great. Thanks. You?"

"Best I've slept since I landed here," responded the captain. "Nice to have company. This island can get pretty lonely."

Angus smiled. He missed his parents but was thankful he'd had Captain Hank for a bunkmate and not one of the stinky pirates aboard the Fearsome Flea. In that regard, walking the plank had turned out to be a stroke of good luck. He settled down on one of the logs around the campfire.

"What's for breakfast?" he asked.

"I'm making grilled crab with flatbread," announced the captain happily. "Coffee?"

Angus nodded. The captain handed him a chipped metal mug. Angus wrapped his hands around it, warming them. He bent his face over the mug and felt the steam tickle his nose. He'd never tried coffee before. It was a drink reserved for adults at his house. He sipped the warm brew eagerly and gagged on the bitter brown liquid.

"Uggh!" He spat out the offensive coffee. It landed in the campfire with a sizzle. He wiped his tongue vigorously up and down his hand trying to remove the taste from his mouth.

"What's the matter?" asked the astonished captain. He took the mug from Angus' hand and gulped it quickly. He looked questioningly at Angus.

"It's so ... yucky!" said Angus lacking adequate words.

"This is a lovely Sumatran, certified organic, fair trade French roast!" said the shocked pirate.

"It's yucky," repeated Angus.

"Several water-tight, shrink-wrapped packages of this washed up in a crate last year. This is my last package! It is an exquisite roast," said the captain.

"It's yucky," Angus persisted.

Captain Hank glared at him and poured himself another cup from the small pot resting beside the campfire.

"I hope you'll have more manners when it comes time to try the crab," he said coldly. "Perhaps you'd like to wash up before we dine?"

Angus shambled off to the water's edge to throw some water on his face and attempt to matt down the hair he knew was sticking up all over his head. He was starting to understand why the crew of the Fearsome Flea had marooned Captain Hank on this island. When he returned to the campfire the small black crow was standing in the sand eagerly breaking crab into small, bite-sized pieces.

"Caw!" she said in greeting and refocused her energies on her breakfast.

Captain Hank's eyes scanned Angus and, apparently approving of what they saw, he handed a dish of crab to the boy. Angus tucked in enthusiastically and immediately yelped.

"Careful. It's hot," said the captain casually.

Angus scowled at him and blew on each piece warily before continuing his meal. The bread was warm and flat, and he used it to scoop up the succulent crab. Within ten minutes, the three hungry friends had devoured every bit of breakfast the captain had prepared. Angus felt warm, satisfied, and rested, and was ready to face the day.

"The fastest route is through the center of the island. Those aren't the best shoes for the job, though." Captain Hank was packing up a sack with provisions. The three friends had decided to hike to the other side of the island and retrieve the tidal booty.

Angus glanced at his flip-flops. He was sure to twist an ankle hiking through the forest in them. He took one off and examined the bottom of his foot. Walking barefoot would be worse. Captain Hank was wearing boots, definitely a good choice of footwear if you were marooned on an uninhabited island.

"Wait! I've got an idea!" announced Angus, and he scurried off to the hut.

He dug through Captain Hank's supply corner, which was remarkably similar to Angus' garage lab table and plastic bins. He pulled out a chunk of white Styrofoam, some rags, fishing net, and two slabs of cedar bark. He laid each flip-flop on top of the Styrofoam and traced a line around them with the tip of his screwdriver. He removed the flip-flops and forced the screwdriver up and down along the outline until he had cut the foam into the shape and size of his shoes.

He placed each piece of cut Styrofoam on top of the cedar bark. Next, he put his flip-flops back on, stood on top of the Styrofoam-bark, and wrapped the fishing net around the layers, lashing the makeshift shoes to his ankles. He shoved rags under the fishing net where it abraded his skin.

Once the shoes were fastened snugly, he took a few steps to try them out. They weren't exactly attractive, but they were springy and solid, and an improvement over flip-flops. He marched back to his friends.

Sitting on the limb of a cedar tree, the little black crow was the first to see him. "Caw-caw-caw-ha-caw," she chuckled. Louder and louder she laughed, "Caw-CAW-HA-CAW." Then the hiccups started, "CAW-CAW-HIC-CAW-CAW-HIC." Her sides puffed in and out as she tried to catch her breath. She began gasping for air in between hiccups. "CAW-HIC-wheeze-CAW-HIC-wheeze." Without warning, the gleeful Ivy fell out of the tree with a tiny thud. A black feather floated silently up.

Angus ignored her, and walked to Captain Hank. The captain glanced at Angus' feet and grunted.

"Well then," he said, furtively shoving the yellow toy duck into the sack before hoisting it to his back. "Ready?"

Angus nodded and the two set off with the bruised but still snickering Ivy in their wake.

Captain Hank and Angus picked their way through the forest and brush. Ivy swooped from tree to tree disappearing now and then to forage for food. Occasionally, the captain would warn Angus to avoid a patch of stinging nettles or to watch his footing over some loose rocks. They stopped once for Angus to readjust his shoes. Neither Angus nor the captain sought conversation. Each was deep in his own thoughts.

The captain was thinking of his mother. His memories of her were softened by time and sweetened by his imagination. She floated in his head like a beautiful, feminine angel. Her face clouded in his mind and was replaced by Maniacal Marge's sneering countenance. He unconsciously clenched his fists as he dreamed up ways to get even with her. He had to get back on his ship. HIS ship, not hers. She had stolen it out from under him, and he would get it back and deal with her. His gait quickened as he grew angrier and angrier.

Next to the silently seething captain, Angus was springing along in his self-made shoes. He loved being out of doors. He did his best thinking in nature. He was feeling quite proud of himself for having made these shoes. And speaking of things to be proud of, how about his Insect Incinerator? He couldn't believe it actually worked! He had to retrieve it and fiddle around with it some more to get it just right. Before he could do that though, he would have to get it back from Marge. He planned to design and build a boat to get back to the Fearsome Flea.

A perfectly shaped walking stick caught his eye and he was quick to grab it. He walked along digging it into the ground as he went, sometimes whacking it against a tree to hear the satisfying thunk, sometimes wielding it in two hands like a broadsword. He swung it to and fro about his head.

"Caw! Hey, watch it!" complained Ivy, who had narrowly avoided being swatted as she flew over Angus' head.

"Sorry," he said reflexively and continued thinking about his boat design. He felt a solution at the edge of his mind. There was something there, just hovering, waiting for him to grasp it. He stopped a moment and bit his bottom lip, considering.

The shapeless fuzz in his brain began to take form. It molded itself into an idea. Suddenly, he knew just what he had to do. "That's it!" he yelled, and raced to the captain. "I've figured it out! How much farther until we get to the beach …" He broke off as he glimpsed the blue-gray of the ocean through the trees. "Quick! Follow me!" He ran off ahead, eager to put his plan into action.

Ivy flapped madly behind him, infected by his excitement. Angus broke through the trees and halted on the ocean-side beach. There was more debris on this side than on the beach facing the sound. Flotsam and jetsam were strewn as far as the eye could see.

"Where is it?" he asked.

"Where is what?" asked Ivy.

"The box of wind-up toys!" Angus spun around frantically scanning the beach.

Ivy flew ahead. "This way."

Angus chased the crow, stumbling over stones as he went. One of his thick cedar-plank shoes became wedged between two rocks, and he landed hard on his right knee.

"Ow!" he yelped, grabbing his knee and rocking back and forth as hot tears sprang to his eyes. He would not cry; he would not cry! Oh, the pain was overwhelming. He felt like laughing and crying at the same time.

Captain Hank appeared at his side and laid his hand gently on Angus' shoulder. "Are you okay?" he asked. He reached a hand down and hauled Angus to his feet. Angus grimaced as he rested his weight on the injured leg.

"I think so," he grunted, fingering the tender spot. "It hurts and tickles at the same time."

"Funny bone," squawked the crow. "Best thing is to keep moving. The minute you sit down and rest it will tense up. It will feel better in a bit. Probably swell up though."

Captain Hank and Angus both looked at her.

"What? I was a human once. Wait right here. I saw some comfrey someplace ..." Ivy glided off toward the forest edge. They watched her slowly circle a patch of weeds and then dive to the ground like a hawk. She flew back to them gripping some leaves in her beak. She fluttered down to Angus' shoulder and placed the leaves in his outstretched hand. "You have to grind these up and wrap them around your knee. It would work better if you made a poultice but that would take more time."

"What will it do?" asked Angus.

"It will help with the bruising," she answered.

Angus and Captain Hank were unconvinced.

"I told you I was good with potions, remember?" asked Ivy. "Trust me."

"Okay," agreed Angus.

"You can grind it faster with a mortar and pestle," said Ivy.

The two humans looked perplexed. Ivy let out an exasperated sigh that came out of her crow voice box as a guttural croak. She fluttered from Angus' shoulder to a small boulder with a divot in the center. "This is a mortar." She tapped her beak on a small, elongated rock. "This is a pestle. You put the comfrey in the mortar and grind it up with the pestle."

Captain Hank took the leaves from Angus and rubbed them between the two rocks. They broke down into a green paste. When Ivy was satisfied with the consistency, she said, "Now you want to spread it on your knee and cover it up. Pack some to bring along. You'll want to reapply it every few hours."

"Turn around," Angus told her. Ivy discreetly turned her back and covered her eyes with a black wing. Angus unfastened his jeans and pulled them down. With the captain's help, Angus applied the sticky powder to his already purpling knee and wrapped a rag around it. Angus pulled his jeans back on and said, "Okay."

Ivy turned around and glanced at Angus. "Fly," she said.

"What?" he asked, and followed her eyes. "Oh," he reddened and quickly zipped up his pants.

The loot Ivy had found on her previous night's exploration was beyond anything Angus could have imagined. It was unbelievable what kind of treasure, his mother would have said garbage, was given up to the ocean. He and the captain had spent the better part of the afternoon searching through the debris and hauling out useful pieces.

Captain Hank had retrieved two pallets of canned peaches, five boxes of variously-sized rusted screws, a beach ball, two salt-bleached buoys, and sundry bits of netting and rope. Angus had whooped with joy when he'd discovered two black plastic animal troughs and a pallet of sneakers. Luckily, the sneakers were only two sizes too large for him. He stuffed them with rags, and considered them an improvement over his Styrofoam shoes. Unluckily, the sneakers only came in two colors: pink and purple. He figured a few well-aimed jumps into a mud puddle would fix that. The rhinestones that covered the shoes would be harder to disguise though.

He laced up his new pink shoes and took a few turns along the beach. He tripped a few times until he learned to lift his knees up a little higher than normal to accommodate the added length of the sneakers. He heard Ivy begin to caw and hiccup as she watched his absurd gait. He hoped she wasn't perched too high off the ground.

Captain Hank rested on a boulder, surrounded by boxes of wind-up toys. His busy hands fiddled with a green plastic frog. "Watch this!" he announced, holding it aloft so Ivy and Angus could see the long frog legs kick in the air. He giggled like a happy child and reached for a long gray shark. "This one's tail moves back and forth! Look!"

"Cool," said the disinterested Angus examining a purple sneaker. Perhaps that color would be easier to camouflage.

The captain grabbed a frog, duck, and shark and ran to the water's edge. He knelt in the surf and wound up the frog and the duck. He lined them up next to each other and watched them paddle to the shore. He wound up the duck and the shark and reran the race. Angus noticed what he was doing and tossed the purple shoe back into its box. He hobbled over to the captain; his knee had stiffened somewhat while he'd been sitting. He picked up the frog and wound it. The captain wound up the duck and the shark again. Without exchanging words Angus and Captain Hank placed all three toys in a line and watched them race to the beach.

"You need to do it again," suggested Ivy. "And I'll keep track of which one wins the most frequently."

"Great idea." Angus wound up the frog again. He and the captain ran the race twenty more times. Ivy made tally marks in the sand with her beak.

"Hmmm. Hardly conclusive," said Angus.

"Do you think we'd have better results in still water?" asked Ivy.

"We might, but we'll be dealing with moving water in our real-life scenario," responded Angus.

"True," agreed Ivy.

The two regarded the sand thoughtfully.

"Excuse me, if you don't mind terribly," interjected the captain. "What are you two talking about?"

"The experiment, of course," answered Angus.

The captain stared at the tally marks blankly.

"The time trial," added Ivy.

"We wanted to know which of the toys would perform best in a certain set of conditions. Which is the fastest? Which has the most powerful propulsion?" said Angus.

"Which one stays wound up longest," said Ivy.

"Oh yes! We forgot to test that," said Angus reaching for the frog and duck. "Captain, if you please." He handed them to the captain and began winding the shark.

Captain Hank took the proffered toys and glanced with uncomprehending eyes from Angus to Ivy. "I still don't understand."

"We need to know which tub toy is the fastest, strongest, and most durable," explained Ivy.

"We're going to use them for the boat's motor," announced Angus.

10

BP Goes to School

BP clambered on to the bus and lumbered to the back. Two girls shared one of the seats and a boy sat alone in the other. The boy regarded BP with a bored expression.

Book bag slung over one shoulder and shoes clasped in his hand, BP growled, "Move."

The boy yawned. "Make me," he said.

BP sighed and rolled his eyes and then clobbered the boy over the head with his shoes. "Move," he repeated more forcefully.

The boy frowned and grabbed the top of his head. "I can't believe you just did that," he gaped. He stood and moved indignantly to another part of the bus. BP grunted and settled himself into the vacated seat.

The two girls stared at him. "That was pretty mean, Angus," said one of them, a slender girl with long, wavy black hair and intelligent brown eyes.

BP wrinkled his nose and snarled at them. "Arrrrr!" One of the girls shrank back into her seat and feigned interest in her fingernails. The black-haired girl wrinkled her forehead and shot him a disapproving look.

"Angus Clark! You are acting like a beast," she declared, crossing her arms and jutting her chin forward. "And you should put on your shoes."

BP narrowed his eyes and gave her his fiercest glare. She returned his look with equal animosity.

The bus pulled to a stop and several riders climbed aboard. "Angus! Dude!" called a cheerful voice. "We sitting in the back today? Cool!"

BP glanced up and saw an energetic boy with short-cropped curly blond hair wobbling along the aisle.

"Avast, matey! Yer eye!" BP pointed in astonishment at the boy's face. It was One-Eyed Billy. In place of an eye patch, Billy now had a healthy eye.

Billy nudged BP to the side, and sat down beside him. "Dude, what happened to your face?" Billy looked equally surprised at BP.

BP raised his hand to his cheek and felt a welt where the cat had scratched him. He'd forgotten about that.

"A midnight fiend tried to kill me. But not to worry. I dealt it a grievous blow. But yer eye, Billy?

What black magic did ye conjure to grow it back?" asked BP.

"Oh cool, are we doing pirates?" asked Billy eagerly.

"Aye, we're pirates, and no mistake. Ye surely ran a rig on me, did ye Billy, ye scallywag!" laughed BP.

"Oh, that explains it," snorted the black-haired girl. "You're pretending to be pirates." She laughed and shook her head dismissively.

"Oh, be quiet, Ivy Calloway. Always thinks she knows better," said Billy. "Right, Angus?"

"I've heard enough 'Angus' to last me fer years," said BP.

"Oh, right," said Billy, becoming serious. "Of course, Angus is too normal. What's your pirate name?"

BP stared at him. "The Booty Poker, of course! Are ye squiffy, mate?"

"Squiffy? No, I don't like that name for me. Yours is really cool though. Funny, too. Booty Poker! I want a good one like that!" said Billy.

BP regarded Billy narrowly. "Why, ye're One-Eyed Billy, of course!"

Billy grabbed his eye. "Cool! I need an eye patch, right?" He opened his lunch box and rifled through its contents. He pulled out a napkin, folded it diagonally, and tied it behind his head. He turned to BP and blinked happily.

"Buffoons," muttered Ivy from the adjacent bus seat.

The bus pulled to a stop.

"Okay, kids. No pushing. Don't forget your bags," called Mr. Nelson.

The children grabbed their bags and books and noisily clambered out of the bus. BP gripped his shoes in one hand and his bag in the other. He looked around in wonderment. This was not the dock! This was nowhere near the water! He'd been tricked! The Fearsome Flea would set sail without him. He turned to Billy.

"We've got to get back to the Fearsome Flea!" he urged.

"The Fearsome Flea?" asked his benapkined friend. "What's that?"

"The scourge of the seven seas. The brutal vessel that casts fear into the very bravest of hearts. Our ship, Billy! Maniacal Marge'll leave without us!" said BP.

"Oh, yeah, right. Our ship. We've got that math test today though. I'll be grounded for a year if I flunk. Maybe we can go after school," Billy turned and hurried into the building.

As BP watched his mate, it suddenly came to him. He remembered this place. Countless hours of fear and torture. More frightening than one thousand midnight fiends. It was a school. He turned on his heel and headed in the opposite direction.

"Angus Clark! Where do you think you're going?" called a stern female voice.

BP spun around and came face to face with a smiling woman sporting a fashionable short hairstyle.

"Did you forget something, Angus? We can call home to your mom. Oh dear, you haven't even put your shoes on this morning. Some mornings are like that, aren't they? Come on inside, and let's get you situated." She hustled him up the steps and into the building. The door closed behind him, and he was trapped inside.

Feet wedged into brown leather shoes, BP shuffled down the hallway from Principal Quigley's office. He couldn't feel the ground beneath his feet and his toes felt pinched. An earsplitting "clang!" startled him and he grabbed his ears.

"Hurry, Angus! That's the bell for first period!" cautioned an adult voice.

BP was quickly remembering how this worked, and he scurried into the first open door he saw and grabbed a seat. He dropped his book bag to the floor. Surprised faces gawked at him.

"Angus, you're not in this class," whispered a heavy-set, freckle-faced boy.

"Angus Clark, I'm thrilled that you enjoy art so much," smiled a fresh-faced woman in a paint-splattered apron. "But I think you have Ms. Evergood this period, don't you?"

BP grunted and stumbled to his feet, swung his bag over his shoulder, and looked around blankly.

"Second floor. Room 24," whispered the freckled boy.

BP winked his eye and gave a quick nod to the boy. "Ye've got me marker, bucko." The boy raised his eyebrows quizzically as BP swaggered from the art room.

He climbed a flight of stairs and scanned the doors for the number 24. There was 20, 22, next one, 24. He pushed open the door and entered the room. In front of him stood a clean, well-groomed, scar-free version of Maniacal Marge.

"So glad you could join us, Angus," said Marge. "Please take your seat and pull out two pencils. I'm about to hand out the test."

BP looked around the room, locked eyes with Billy, and walked confidently toward him.

"Your seat, Angus," called Marge. BP stopped and turned. "Beside Ivy, please," said Marge.

The dark-haired girl from the bus wiggled her fingers and smiled sweetly at him. He lifted his lip in a sneer and threw himself into the seat beside her.

"Pencil, Angus," whispered Ivy. "Oh, I mean 'Booty Poker'." She giggled. He crossed his arms and fixed her with a hard stare. She raised her hand. "Ms. Evergood? I think Angus may need a pencil."

"Why doesn't that surprise me?" sighed Ms. Evergood.

11

Making Glue

Captain Hank and Angus piled the booty into the two black plastic animal troughs to transport it back to the camp on the eastern beach. Angus broke apart several pallets and fastened them to the bottom of the troughs to create some land skis. They tethered the troughs one behind the other with a pull rope on the front one. They each grabbed a piece of rope.

"Oof," grunted Captain Hank as he tugged, moving the trough train a few inches. Angus pulled with all his might. His knee throbbed, and his head hurt from holding his breath, but the train didn't budge.

"Why don't you try working together?" Ivy piped up. "On the count of three. One, two, three!"

With a large grunt, the two humans pulled, moving the train another inch.

"It's not working," said the captain.

"What if we use the technology of the Iditarod?" suggested Angus.

"Could try. Probably won't have much effect but it's worth a shot," replied Ivy, perching on the front trough.

"What?" asked the captain. "The idea rod?"

"No, no, the Iditarod," explained Ivy as Angus got to work tying a series of harnesses into the rope. "It's a famous dog sled race in Alaska. Between six and eight dogs are tied to a towline attached to a sled. The weight of the sled is distributed across the dogs, so they're able to pull together what they couldn't pull alone."

"Okay, let's give it a try." Angus stepped between the two ropes he had attached to the trough sleds. He fastened the harness around his torso. The captain watched him closely and then put on his harness in the same way.

"On the count of three," croaked Ivy. "One, two, three!"

Instead of using just their arms, Angus and Captain Hank leaned their entire bodies into the harness. The trough train slid painfully forward, a little farther than before, until Angus gasped, "I need to stop."

He put his hands on his knees and bent his head low, gulping air. Captain Hank huffed from a standing position and said, "This isn't going to work."

The crow cocked her head thoughtfully. "How about if you untie one of the troughs?"

Captain Hank unfastened his harness. He walked to the rope that secured the back and front troughs to each other, selected a tool on his Swiss army knife, and used it to loosen the knot. The rope fell away. He walked to Angus, laid his hand on the boy's back, and asked, "Feeling okay?"

"Better. Thanks."

The pirate refastened his harness and said, "Anytime you're ready, Angus."

Angus took a deep breath, and stood upright. He exhaled loudly. "Count us off, Ivy."

"One, two, three!" The lightened sled began to scrape over the rocks. The rush of excitement Angus felt at its comparatively rapid movement translated into a surge of energy. Angus trudged along behind the gangly captain, towing the packed trough across the rocky beach. The pallet skis attached to the bottom caught on jutting sticks several times. The weight and momentum of the sled loosened the sticks and carried them along.

When they arrived at the forest's edge, Captain Hank stopped. They faced a three-foot incline into the wooded terrain.

"Let's rest a moment," panted the captain.

"Sounds good to me!" Angus leaned against the trough and watched the captain stretch his arms behind his back and shake out his legs. The captain wandered down the beach toward the incoming tide and gazed back toward the forest. He looked up to the sky, thought for a moment, and strolled back to where Angus and Ivy waited.

"This isn't going to work," he declared.

"What do you mean? Look how far we've come!" said Angus.

"Look at the sun." Captain Hank pointed to the sky. It was beginning to glow orange as the sun slipped closer to the horizon. "We'll be lucky if we can haul this thing back to camp by the morning. And I, for one, do not intend to march through the forest in the dark tied to this thing."

Angus began to protest but Ivy interrupted him. "Captain Hank is right. How are you going to drag this thing through the forest, around trees, up and down hills? And then you'll have to come back tomorrow and drag the other one, too." She quirked her head in the direction of the second trough they had untied.

Angus considered what his friends had said. He peered into the trough. It would be lighter if they unloaded it, but they needed all the supplies they had packed inside it. And even if the trough weighed less and was easier to move, it would still be difficult to squeeze it between some of those trees they'd hiked past this morning. As much as he hated to admit it, his friends were right. It wasn't going to work.

"So does either of you have a better idea?" he asked.

"You could build the boat here on this beach," said Ivy.

Angus stood dumbstruck for a moment, and then slapped himself on the forehead. "Of course! Why didn't I think of that?" It was so elementary, he was embarrassed it hadn't occurred to him.

Captain Hank agreed. "I suggest we pack up some food supplies and hike back to East Beach before it gets any darker," he said, reaching into the trough and retrieving his pack. He unzipped it and began stuffing cans into it.

"Let's leave everything else here," suggested Angus. "Tomorrow morning, we can hike back with some tools to build the boat."

After Captain Hank and Angus had packed everything they could carry, they strode briskly into the forest. On the way, Angus trod through every mud puddle he could find. That evening, his wet, brown sneakers dried by the fire. Ivy couldn't resist trying to pluck off the glittering rhinestones.

The next day, they returned to West Beach. Besides lunch they had packed the captain's metal soup pot and matches. Angus' trusty screwdriver hung in its usual position around his neck. His safety goggles rested on his forehead. The captain built a small fire on the beach and warmed a pot of coffee.

As Ivy hopped excitedly from driftwood log to Angus' shoulder to trough rim, Angus and the captain built the boat that they hoped would carry them off the island. They planned to build the boat close to the tidal plain so they wouldn't have to struggle to get it into the water.

Together, they maneuvered the troughs to rest side by side. They found two large logs of nearly the same length and width. They each took an end.

"Now, lift!" commanded Captain Hank.

Angus strained, grunting loudly. His end of the log rose two inches off the ground, then slipped from his hand and thudded back to the beach. If he hadn't reacted quickly the heavy driftwood would have landed on his foot.

"What happened?" asked the captain, easing the log back to the beach.

"I got a splinter," said Angus, examining the palm of his hand.

"You don't drop a heavy log simply because you've got a splinter! What kind of man are you?" the captain blustered.

"I didn't drop the log because of a splinter!" Angus replied indignantly. "I got a splinter because I dropped the log. And I'm not a man! The log is too heavy for me to lift."

The captain was flabbergasted. "Yes, of course," he muttered sheepishly. "Of course you aren't yet a man. I'll drag it over myself."

Angus was always so sure of himself. He had planned the escape from the island. The boat design was completely his idea. He was such a capable person that the captain had completely forgotten he was still a boy.

Angus returned his focus to his injured hand. "Let me see it," croaked Ivy. "Yikes, that is a big one." She cocked her head and regarded the splinter with one eye. "Bring it closer. Rest your hand on that rock, right there. I think I can get it." Ivy opened her beak and promptly bit Angus' palm.

"Ouch!" yelled Angus, snatching his hand away and glaring at Ivy. "What did you do that for?"

"Sorry. I missed. I thought I could grab the splinter," explained Ivy. "Let me try again."

"No way." Angus hid his hand protectively behind his back while looking distrustfully at the crow.

"I promise I won't try to pull it out again with my beak. I'll scratch it out," encouraged Ivy.

"Oh yeah, that sounds a lot better," said Angus sarcastically.

"Your hand could get infected if you don't get the splinter out," Ivy went on. "It will become red, and hot and swollen, and then the infection will spread to your wrist and your elbow, and before you know it you'll have gangrene and rotting skin and your whole arm will be yellow and filled with pus."

They heard a gagging sound and looked up from their argument to see the decidedly nauseous captain retching on to the beach. "Just let her do it," he said, wiping his mouth. "The alternative sounds ghastly."

Glaring fiercely, Angus warily rested his hand on the rock beside the small crow. He squeezed his eyes shut and held his breath. He felt some scraping across his palm. "It's out," said Ivy. She puffed herself up proudly and fluffed out her feathers. He brought his hand to his face. Except for a tiny hole and a few flakes of skin there was no evidence a splinter had ever been there.

"Thanks," he said.

"Don't mention it." She cawed and flew off into the forest.

"I could use your help over here," called Captain Hank, standing beside the troughs. "Think you can help me hoist the logs?"

"Well, if you rest that end there and push this one up here." Angus walked over to help.

Ivy returned to find two logs lashed across the top of the adjoining animal troughs. Angus was sorting through the wind-up toys while Captain Hank fed the campfire. "That looks sturdy." She nodded toward the boat.

"Just trying to find a way to attach these stupid things to the stern," Angus mumbled, growing frustrated. He grabbed a wind-up frog and chucked it at the ocean.

"Calm down," soothed Captain Hank, reverently picking up the frog. "Why don't you step away from it for a while? I'll warm up a can of chili for lunch. Go take a walk or something."

Angus shoved the toys out of his way and stood. He stomped along the beach angrily kicking stones and pebbles and muttering to himself. "Stupid, dumb, boat. Stinking toys. Dumb idea. Stupid, stupid."

They could always build oars and paddle through the ocean to the Fearsome Flea. A mast and sail wouldn't be too hard to construct either. But neither of those solutions was worthy of Angus Clark, Inventor-in-Training. This toy motor thing just had to work.

As he walked along, one thing became abundantly clear. He had to go to the bathroom. He headed into the cover of the trees. He hiked into the brush where he was sure he would not be seen by a certain curious crow. He relieved himself and fumbled with his pants. As he was about to zip he was startled by a loud "CAW! CAW!" overhead. He stumbled forward and braced himself against a cedar tree. He looked angrily up, saw a brazen crow peering down at him, and sighed with relief when he realized it was just a crow, not Ivy.

He rubbed his hands together and was dismayed to find that they were sticky with sap from the tree. He hated tree sap! You could never get it off. No matter how much soap and hot water you used it remained on your hands for days. Just one more annoyance to deal with. His mood completely soured, he hiked back out of the forest.

"Lunch is ready!" called the captain.

Angus walked back to the campfire. He ran his hands distractedly through his hair and groaned. Now he had tree sap in his hair! If his mother could see him now he could just imagine what she would say. And as he considered how much it would hurt to try to get a comb through his unruly hair, it dawned on him.

"That's it! Tree sap! We'll make glue from tree sap!"

Captain Hank grinned, watching Angus dance back and forth gleefully singing, "Tree sap, tree sap!"

"Angus, I'm so glad you've figured it out," droned the crow. "I never had any doubt in your ability to solve the problem. But for the sake of all of us, won't you please, please, zip up your fly?"

Angus tugged at his zipper and frantically spun in circles. "I need something to collect the tree sap." Before the captain had time to react, Angus snatched the pot off the fire and dumped its contents on to the beach.

"No!" yelled Captain Hank, but Angus had already set off sprinting to the forest. Ivy flew ahead of him rapidly scanning the trees for scarring.

"Caw! Caw! Caw!" she announced, landing on a dead bough. "Try here!" She pointed her beak at a tree with a fresh wound.

Angus took the screwdriver from around his neck and poked it into the tree's injury unplugging the clogged sap. "It's going too slowly!"

"Here, use this," said the captain, having followed them to the forest. He handed Angus his army knife. He knew that he wouldn't be eating his lunch until the boy had satisfied his curiosity.

Angus reached back and grabbed the tool. He flicked through each utensil on the knife, probing until he found one that satisfied him. He selected a corkscrew and drilled it into the tree as deep as it would go, unscrewed it, and drilled again. "It's not working!"

"Let me try," suggested the captain and Angus grudgingly complied. The captain selected a simple blade and patiently carved into the tree. After several minutes, sap began to flow sluggishly. The captain stepped back, crossed his arms, and admired his work.

"That's no faster!" said Angus.

"It's not about speed," said the captain. "It's about quantity." He strode back towards the beach.

"What?" Ivy and Angus said in unison.

"We need more containers," the captain shouted back. "We have to drill into more trees."

After the friends had collected enough sap in multiple containers to fill the captain's pot, Angus was ready to make glue. The captain noticed the daylight was beginning to wane. Angus didn't want to wait another day to find out whether or not his glue would work, so Captain Hank hiked back to East Beach to collect supplies for sleeping at West Beach. While Angus waited for him to return, he stoked the fire and nestled the pot of sap amidst the hot coals. He squatted down and began to stir the sap slowly with a long, thin stick. The sap bubbled and sputtered.

His right arm rapidly grew tired. He alternated hands but his left arm fatigued even sooner. He switched back and forth between hands. When he thought he couldn't possibly stir anymore, he held the stick with both hands. He could feel blisters beginning to swell up along his palms. He needed a break, just a little one. He sat back from the fire, stretched his arms and aching back, and decided to cool his hands in the water lapping at the shore.

The icy water felt delicious on his raw palms. He closed his eyes and enjoyed the slow numbing sensation.

"CRAAAK!" His eyes flew open and he spun around at the horrific noise. A small black crow lay by the side of the fire, feathers steaming and scorched, molten sap running down its motionless body.

"Ivy!" Angus shrieked and raced to her.

He had left the sap cooking unattended over the fire. It was jumping and popping in the pot. It must have gotten too hot and exploded. Exploded all over Ivy. He grabbed the pot handle and pulled it off the coals, burning his fingertips. Then he tenderly picked up the little black body. Its neck hung limp in his hand. Its eyes were glazed and gray, a sharp contrast to the bright, intelligent, black eyes he was used to seeing. The small chest lay still.

"No! Ivy! No!" Angus sobbed, tears coursing down his cheeks. He gathered the little crow to his chest, and held it against his heart, as if its beating could make hers begin again, like a jumper cable between two car engines. His vision clouded by tears, he looked down at her body. "My fault. All my fault. I'm so sorry, Ivy. So terribly sorry. My wonderful friend. Ivy." He closed his eyes and kissed the top of her feathery head.

12

Chef's Surprise

BP strutted into the cafeteria with Billy. By slyly copying off of Ivy's paper, he had dispatched the math test quickly. He had purposely dropped his paper when Ms. Evergood came around to collect them. When she bent over to pick it up off the floor, he had raised his pencil to strike. Ivy had grabbed his wrist and mouthed "No!", and he had missed his opportunity.

The next period had introduced him to a mustachioed man with glasses named Mr. Stevenson who'd asked the class to write their impressions of a one-legged pirate named Long John Silver. BP had neither met nor heard of that particular scallywag, so he scrawled down his memory of Shep's brother Jake, who'd lost his finger in a small explosion while he was cleaning the cannon. BP had been swabbing the deck at the time and remembered the burst of fire, and the detached digit flying through the air and landing on the deck with a splat. Jake had screamed "Me finger! Me finger!" BP had bent down to retrieve the bloody digit but a seagull dove out of the riggings, grabbed the severed member in its bill, and flew off. The finger was never seen again, and Jake was dubbed Mr. Stumpy. Mr. Stevenson had given him an odd look when he'd read the paper.

Then had come art class, and BP had put his deck-swabbing skills to good use. He was still a little wobbly on land, and when the floor started to sway, he grabbed his easel to steady himself. The easel toppled to the side, struck Billy's easel standing beside his, which struck Ivy's standing next to that, and so on, like a row of dominoes. His classmates stared at him shocked, scowling, and paint-spattered. Because he alone was not drenched with paint, it fell to him to mop the floor while the others went to wash.

And now he was ready to eat.

"I'm starved!" he crowed. "Take me to the grub!"

"Aye, aye, matey," answered Billy. He held up his lunch box. "I'll grab us a table while you get your meal."

BP followed the children who were standing in line waiting for a warm meal. He craned his neck forward to see what was being served. One woman in a hairnet sliced pepperoni and cheese pizzas and divided them up among the eagerly waiting students. Another hair-netted woman stared straight ahead with a bored expression on her face. She clutched a ladle and stirred a large, steaming cook pot. The students kept their distance from her like pirates avoiding the Fearsome Flea's head on cleaning day.

BP recognized the freckle-faced boy from art class and stood behind him in the lunch line.

"What's she got in there?" he asked, pointing to the large cauldron.

"Chef's Surprise." The boy made a vomiting noise. "They take everything left over from the week before and mix it together. It's disgusting."

BP watched anxiously as another pizza was brought out and cut into slices. He was nearing the front of the line but there were still at least ten students in front of him.

"This is the last one, kids," called the pizza lady as she sliced into the pizza. The line began to pulse as the children realized that many of them would be left to eat the dubious Chef's Surprise.

BP counted: One student, two students, how many slices of pizza were left? From his count, the freckle-faced boy would get the last piece! He wasn't that big. BP reasoned it was worth a try to fight him for it. He muscled his way in front of him.

"Hey! You cut the line!" protested the boy, shoving him.

"Did not!" said BP, shoving back.

"Did too!" said the boy, punching BP in the arm.

"No fighting!" A shrill voice rebuked them. The boys left off pushing each other and turned to see Ivy marching determinedly toward them. "What are we? Animals?"

"It's my turn next. It's my slice!" the boy appealed to Ivy.

"There's no way I'll be eatin' from that cauldron of filth!" argued BP.

Ivy shrugged her shoulders at the two squabbling boys and said, "Looks like you're both having Chef's Surprise today." They spun around and watched the next child in line, who had been waiting patiently while they quarreled, walk off with the last pizza slice.

Lunch was beyond repulsive, and this from a pirate who was used to eating lumpy oat bits and watered down salmon stock. The Chef's Surprise was chunky and glutinous. There were specks of something black, and a slimy green seaweed-like vegetable spread throughout. BP closed his eyes, took a nibble and tried to swallow, but the texture alone made him gag. He glared at Ivy sitting across the room with several girls complacently chewing a carrot. If she hadn't distracted him, he might have been able to snatch that last piece of pizza.

Billy looked sympathetically at him. "Dude, that is really gross. You can't possibly eat that. Here, have some of my sandwich."

"Mate, that is right kind of ye," said BP taking a bite of the bologna and American cheese Billy offered. He clapped him on the shoulder. "Ye've always been a good mate to me, and I willna forget it. I'll stand beside ye in battle any day."

Billy looked embarrassed. "Dude, it's just a sandwich. Here, have some chips."

BP savored the salty crispness of the fried potatoes.

"Hey, Angus." BP looked up and narrowed his eyes at Ivy who hovered over him. "How's your lunch?"

"What do ye think?" he growled.

"I just wanted you to know, so you're not surprised when you get your math grade," said Ivy.

"Know what?" asked BP crunching a chip.

"I saw you copying off of me, so I wrote down all the wrong answers. That means, you flunked your math test," she said.

BP shrugged. He didn't care. He was a pirate. He'd be going back to the Fearsome Flea where no one did math. But Billy was shocked.

"But then you got them all wrong too, Ivy," said Billy.

"I told Ms. Evergood, and she let me fix it right after class," said Ivy. "I'm surprised at you Angus. You knew that math backwards and forwards. Why did you cheat?"

"I told ye! My name's BP, not Angus, and I've need of a good dagger, a bit of plunder, and a warm meal, not math!" said BP.

"Whatever. Stick with your silly pirate story. I just wanted you to know," sighed Ivy walking back to her table.

"Angus, I mean Booty Poker, this is not good dude, not good at all," Billy shook his head solemnly.

"It doesna matter, One Eye. We'll be aboard the Fearsome Flea before the day is out," responded BP cheerfully. "No need for math on the high seas."

"Dude, this is a fun game and all, but get real. Your mom is gonna freak out when she sees that grade. Worse if Ms. Evergood tells her you cheated. You really shouldn't have copied off Ivy. You are gonna be grounded until you're twenty," said Billy.

BP laughed and looked uncomprehendingly at Billy. "You've run a good rig on me One-Eye. But enough of the joke. Let's get to the dock." He poked around in his bag until he found Mrs. Clark's earrings. He poked a hoop through each ear lobe, and tightened the diamond studs in the two remaining holes.

Billy stared at him. "Wow, you are really taking this pirate thing far. Does your mom know you're wearing her jewelry?"

Just then, the freckle-faced boy walked past the table carrying his bowl of Chef's Surprise. He moved to one side to let a girl pass and jostled BP's hand causing him to tug painfully on his ear.

"Watch yerself, ye bilge rat!" snarled BP pushing him away.

"Who you calling a bilge rat, line cutter?" the boy responded, pushing back. The bowl dropped out of his hand and bits of the glutinous mass spilled on BP's leg.

BP looked down at the Chef's Surprise staining his pant leg. It was revolting. He didn't know how landlubbers got even, but he sure knew how pirates did. He reached into his own bowl, pulled out a particularly nasty glob of cold seaweed, and hurled it in the boy's general direction. Unfortunately, he missed.

"Hey!" yelled a short boy munching on an apple at the next table as he wiped the mess from his glasses. He picked up his neighbor's glass of milk and lobbed it toward BP. The milk splashed down the front of a girl walking to the garbage with her tray. She shrieked and dumped the remnants of her lunch on a large boy at another table, who up until that moment had been belching the alphabet. He hooted happily and threw handfuls of Chef's Surprise in every direction.

This commenced the first all-school food fight that had ever occurred on Principal Quigley's watch. Lunch was thrown, floors were mopped, parents were called, and BP spent a very uncomfortable fifteen minutes riding home in a car with the white-faced and fuming Mrs. Clark.

The next day, a decree was handed down from the office of the principal that Chef's Surprise would never again be served for lunch.

13

Body Jumping

"Ow! That really hurt!"

Angus looked at the limp crow body in his hand. He could have sworn he'd heard Ivy's voice.

"You could have killed me, you know! What were you thinking? Leaving the glue on the fire like that?" Angus squeezed his eyes shut, and then opened them and stared at the crow carcass. Apparently he was so crazy with grief he was now hearing voices.

"Put that corpse down. You'll have to bury it later. Poor valiant animal sacrificed its life for science," continued Ivy's voice.

Angus placed the crow body gently beside the fire, wiped his eyes, and looked expectantly around. "Ivy?"

"Over here ... three steps forward, two to the right. Watch your feet! You almost stepped on me! Down here!" instructed the bossy voice.

Angus squatted down and looked at the ground. "Where are you?"

"Right here! You're too far away. Come closer," the voice ordered.

Angus knelt down and examined the rocks. "I still don't see you." A tiny jet of water sprayed him in the eye. He blinked and reached down to gently extract a tiny off-white and brown clam from the wet sand between the beach pebbles. He gripped it between his fingers and held it close to his eyes. "Ivy, is that you?"

"If it isn't, you sure look ridiculous talking to a clam," she retorted.

Tears sprang to his eyes again as he realized his friend was alive. He hadn't killed her after all.

"Don't go crying all over me! There's salt in your tears and they sting," the clam scolded.

"Sorry, Ivy. I'm just so glad you're still here. When I saw you lying there by the fire ..." His throat constricted with emotion, and he was unable to continue.

"Well, I was going to yell at you about that but seeing how sorry you are, I guess I forgive you," said Ivy. "You're going to have to bury that body, though. It freaks me out to see it lying there. Kind of like seeing myself in the hospital bed hooked up to machines all over again."

"But how did you survive?" asked Angus.

"I don't really know. The last thing I remember is peeking down into the pot to see how the glue was coming along, then this searing, hot pain, worst thing I've ever felt in my life, and the next thing I know I was watching you and my old body from a distance."

"You saved yourself by jumping from one body to another." Angus whistled. "That is pretty cool."

"The weird thing is that I didn't consciously try to body jump. I don't remember doing anything," said Ivy.

"So either you've gotten so good at body jumping you can do it without thinking, or ..." Angus trailed off.

"Or my mind can't stay in a body that's dead." Ivy was really thinking now. "I've never tried to transport my mind into anything non-living. Hold on a second."

It was hard to tell what Ivy was doing because the little hard shell just sat there. Angus imagined it must be pretty boring to be a clam.

"Nothing," Ivy's voice said. "I tried to move into a rock, and then a log, but I just stayed a clam. Then I tried to go back into the crow body. Nothing. What do you think that means?"

"Well, your mind won't allow you to stay in a dead crow and you can't move into a non-living entity. Have you ever tried moving into a human?" asked Angus.

"I've only tried to move into myself in the different worlds," answered Ivy. "It never occurred to me to try someone else."

"Try me!" Angus suggested impulsively.

"Think about it a minute," said Ivy. "If I went into your body, where would you go?"

Angus hadn't thought about that. Now it worried him. "I don't know."

"Too dangerous. I'm afraid we wouldn't get you back, and I don't want to go through life as a boy," said Ivy.

Angus was relieved. "Yeah. I kind of like my body. Not sure I'd want to trade places with you in that clamshell."

"So does that mean," began Ivy.

"You can't die in an animal body?" finished Angus. "But how could you know for sure?"

"Well, you could put me on the ground and stomp on me," suggested the clam.

"But what if we're wrong? Then I would have your murder on my conscience forever. I couldn't live with that," said Angus.

"True. And it would really hurt," said the clam. "I guess we'll just have to wait and see if I survive the next time you accidentally kill me."

The clam spurted water. Angus suspected Ivy was laughing at him.

"Not funny," he scowled. "Now what? You're a clam. What do we do about that? Should I stick you in my pocket?"

"No way I'm living in your pocket! Gross! You've probably got snotty tissues and chewed gum in there. I've got to find another animal body. Can you walk down the beach and put me on the sand? Far from the fire, and then walk away. I've got an idea," said the clam.

Angus wasn't sure what Ivy was up to but he complied and walked until Ivy told him to stop. "Here's as good a place as any," she said. He placed her on the ground and walked back to the fire. While he waited, he picked up the cooling pot and examined the cedar sap. It was thick and sticky. He picked up a pebble, dabbed a bit of the glue on it, and stuck another pebble to it. He squeezed them together for a few moments. When he let go they stayed together. He gave them a gentle tug, but they resisted. The glue appeared to be a success.

Angus looked up from the pebbles and gazed down the beach. The tide was coming in and with it several seabirds. He watched as a gray and white gull soared over the beach in lazy circles. It dove toward the beach, and Ivy. "No!" yelled Angus dropping the pebbles and setting off in great strides down the beach. He waved his hands around his head and screamed, "Shoo! Shoo! Get out of here you filthy flying rat!"

"Who are you calling a flying rat?" shrieked the gull. "I find such comparisons very insulting."

"Ivy! You're a gull now? I thought that gull, I mean you, was going to eat you, I mean the clam," stuttered Angus. All this body jumping was making his head hurt.

"The gull would have eaten the clam but that was the whole point. I needed the gull to get close enough to the clam so I could move into its body. I can't jump bodies if the animal is too far away," said Ivy. "I guess the clam must have been the nearest living thing to the fire when my crow body died. And I couldn't stay a clam. I have to be able to move."

Angus wondered if he'd been close to the campfire rather than far away at the water's edge when the glue exploded all over Ivy, would she be in his body now? He shuddered and shook his head to dispel the thought.

While Ivy watched in her new seagull body, Angus dug a hole in the ground beyond the tide's reach. He placed the crow carcass gently in the hole and looked to Ivy. "Should we say a few words?" he asked.

"Thank you, crow, for allowing me to inhabit your body. I'm sorry you died," said Ivy.

"Is that enough?" asked Angus.

"Feel free to add to it," answered Ivy.

Angus gazed blankly at the crumpled body. After a few moments of silence he said, "Amen." He looked to Ivy. She nodded her head and began pushing sand into the hole with her orange bill. Angus compressed the sand with the palm of his hand. When they had refilled the hole, Angus gathered flat, smooth rocks, and stacked them on top of one another in order of size, largest at the bottom. He stepped back and admired his work.

"A cairn. Nice touch," Ivy approved.

"Thought it was the least I could do," said Angus.

"What's going on?" asked Captain Hank walking out of the forest with several blankets over his arm and a pack of food strapped to his back.

Angus and the seagull looked at each other. "He'll never understand," Ivy whispered.

"Oh, just taking a break," said Angus. "Let me show you the glue. It turned out great!"

He led Captain Hank to the fireside and the pot of glue.

14

Discipline

Mrs. Clark was fond of repeating the adage that both good things and bad things happen in threes. This was indeed the case on the day of the food fight.

Bad Thing Number One. After running behind the bus with her absentminded son's shoes, she returned to her front door and discovered that Mr. Clark had left for work and locked the door securely behind him.

She stood in front of her home dressed in her tatty bathrobe and slovenly lime sherbet slippers unsure how to get back in to the house. She paced around it, turning door knobs, tugging on windows, trying to locate one that was unlocked. She stepped back and looked up at her home, which would be so much cozier if she could just get inside.

Good Thing Number One. On the second floor, she noticed Angus' bedroom window. He had forgotten to close it before leaving for school. If she could just reach it, she could climb through it and be back in her cozy house.

However, the garage door was locked, so there was no getting at a ladder.

Good Thing Number Two. Beneath the bedroom window stood a small peach tree. The tree's peaches had long since been harvested and eaten and its limbs reached out to her and beckoned for her to climb them.

In her youth, she had been the most fearless and fastest tree climber in her neighborhood, boy or girl. Throughout her childhood her friends could often be seen standing beneath the oldest and tallest trees gazing into the branches and holding stop watches. She had wanted to get into the Guinness Book of World Records and had nearly achieved her dream. By the time she was fourteen though, she'd given up her quest for more age-appropriate pastimes. Now, Mrs. Clark scrambled eagerly up the peach tree, reliving her glory days and forgetting that she was now middle-aged.

She suddenly remembered this when she found the front half of her body wedged in Angus' window while the back half kicked helplessly behind her.

Mr. Siegfried, the spry octogenarian at the end of the street, kept his mind and body young by walking around the block three times a day. His first walk occurred directly after his breakfast of a soft boiled egg, half a grapefruit, and a cup of black tea. He shuffled off with purpose, eyes focused down on the uneven pavement.

Good Thing Number Three. The morning of the food fight, Mr. Siegfried uncharacteristically happened to glance up into the sky to gauge the day's weather at the very moment that Mrs. Clark waved one of her green slippers off her foot.

The law-abiding elderly citizen shambled back to his home and phoned the police. A uniformed man helped Mrs. Clark into her home, asked her several probing and embarrassing questions, and respectfully refrained from outward signs of humor until he was seated again in his patrol car.

And with that, the three good things were all used up.

Freshly showered and dressed, Mrs. Clark stumbled over her son's forgotten school books. She sighed, grabbed her jacket, and set out for the garage with the books and her car keys. She was surprised to see the hatchback held open by one of Angus' "inventions". To her untrained eye, it looked like an old fishing pole tethered to a broken bread machine. She tossed the invention to his disheveled corner of the messy garage, closed the hatchback, climbed into the car, and put her keys into the ignition.

Bad Thing Number Two. She turned her keys expecting the engine to cough and then start. It didn't.

The emergency technician who showed up an hour later explained that the interior lights, triggered by the open hatchback, had drained the engine's battery. After he installed a new one and charged her credit card, Mrs. Clark set off for Angus' school with the books.

Mrs. Clark smiled to herself as she re-entered her cozy home. She planned to bake a chocolate cake this afternoon. If she finished it quickly, she'd be able to cut herself a sugary, thick slice before Angus returned from school.

She had forgotten that bad things happen in threes.

Mrs. Clark was accustomed to calls from Principal Quigley. Mrs. Clark was an active member of the school's parent and teacher association. She was the first to sign up for bake sales and class parties. She sat up past midnight every spring sewing costumes for the annual all-school musical. Whenever Principal Quigley needed a parent to support the school's efforts, rally other parents to volunteer, or head up a new committee, Mrs. Clark's phone would ring. And since Mrs. Clark prized good citizenship and an excellent education above almost everything else in life, she always answered.

Principal Quigley requested that Mrs. Clark return to the school she had just left to retrieve her son. His presence would not be requested at school for the next few days.

Bad Thing Number Three. Mrs. Clark, costume designer and bake sale diva, upstanding parental citizen with a speed dial position on the school principal's phone, was now the mother of a suspended student.

The stony silence inside the car on the drive home unnerved BP.

When he messed up on the Fearsome Flea punishment was fast and loud. Maniacal Marge would yell at the top of her lungs. Depending on the severity of the infraction, BP would be given extra chores, cuffed on the ear, swatted on the behind, or threatened with plank-walking or keel-hauling.

Mrs. Clark's displeasure was much more terrifying.

She parked the car and climbed out, slamming the door. Without bothering to look back to see if BP was behind her, she entered the house. BP sat in the car for a moment, listening to the engine ping and pong as it cooled down. He pictured Mrs. Clark pinging and ponging as she cooled down. Maybe he should just wait it out in safety here in the car.

He laughed at himself. What was he worried about anyway? He was a fierce pirate after all and had faced the raging tirades of Maniacal Marge.

This pink-lipsticked mother was certainly no scarier than that!

He grabbed his book bag and got out of the car. He walked to the door, pulled it open, and peeked inside. Mrs. Clark bustled about the kitchen pulling mixing bowls and baking ingredients off of shelves and out of cupboards. The door slammed behind BP, and he dropped his bag to the floor. Mrs. Clark ignored him.

She was acting much differently than he'd expected. The mother he'd known before he'd run off to join the pirates would have raged and railed at him for his behavior at school. Who was this woman standing before him? None of it mattered anyway. It was past time for him to return to the Fearsome Flea.

"Well, I'll be on me way," he spoke tentatively.

Mrs. Clark thumbed through a cookbook.

"Did ye hear me? I'll be headin' back to me ship," he said a bit louder.

Mrs. Clark turned some knobs on the oven.

"Me ship is sure to leave harbor soon. Don't want to miss her." He picked his bag up off the floor.

Mrs. Clark began measuring ingredients and pouring them into a mixing bowl.

BP put his hand on the door knob, and tried one last time. "Well ... bye."

Without raising her eyes from the eggs she was beating Mrs. Clark said, "You are welcome to leave any time you like, but you'll do so with your property, not mine."

BP stopped and stuttered, "I don't know what ye mean."

Mrs. Clark raised her eyes to his. "Take off my earrings," she commanded.

BP raised his hand to his ears and removed the jewelry.

"And I'll have my salt shaker," she said.

He tried to look innocent.

She pointed with a dripping whisk. "In the bag."

He sighed, unzipped the book bag, and drew out the salt shaker.

"Come to think of it that bag stays here. I bought it, so that makes it mine," she said.

He shrugged and opened the door.

"Oh, and the clothes you're wearing," she said.

He spun around and gaped at her.

Her lips curled in a smile that did not meet her eyes. "Those belong to me, too. Leave them here before you go."

"But that's indecent!" he protested.

She returned her attention to the recipe book. BP started out the door.

"Clothes," she ordered.

He stopped, turned back around, and re-entered the kitchen.

"I can't walk naked through the streets!" he croaked.

"Well, you won't be walking anywhere in my property. You own what you came into this world with," she said. She looked at him. "If you choose to leave, you may go as God made you. If, on the other hand, you choose to continue living under our roof, eating our food, and wearing our clothes, you will abide by our rules. And one of them is to not get suspended from school. Now which is it?"

BP thought a moment. He would be the laughing stock of the Fearsome Flea if he showed up naked. If he just waited it out a bit longer, he could sneak away when Mrs. Clark least expected it. Marge had been at the school today, so chances were the ship was still docked.

He nodded at Mrs. Clark. "Stay," he said.

"Then go to your room and wait for your father to get home," said Mrs. Clark as she began mixing the cake batter.

15

The Boat

After a chilly, uncomfortable night sleeping in the
open at West Beach, Angus and Captain Hank
began adding the finishing touches to the animal
trough boat. After determining that the salt water
would not degrade the cedar sap glue, they painted
it on to the stern and applied three rows of wind-up
toys grouped by type.

The frogs had the longest legs, which Angus
thought would be most useful at a deeper water
level, so they were on the bottom row. The sharks,
with their short but strong side-to-side tail motion,

were placed in the middle. The captain thought ducks should sit on top of the water. The yellow ducks and their splashing paddles were glued along the top.

They quickly ran out of glue, so the captain gathered more sap from the trees they had tapped the day before and began to cook it down. Angus had explained what had happened to the crow to impress upon Captain Hank not to leave the cedar sap unsupervised over the campfire. After meeting the talking seagull, the captain was more convinced than ever that Angus was a world-class animal trainer. Angus and Ivy didn't even try to explain what had really happened.

While the captain was occupied with the glue, Angus began trying to solve the problem of keeping the wind-up toys wound. Ivy sat beside him on the beach as he fiddled with various found objects and talked to himself. She was learning that Angus did a lot of his thinking out loud.

"The rope would be easy to hold on to in the boat, but it's too thick to wrap around the knobs," Angus mumbled. "No, it won't work. Stupid, stupid. String? Still too big ... need something smaller. Rubber bands! Aha, yes! And string after ..."

Ivy knew he'd figured out a solution when his eyes began to gleam and he shouted, "I've got it!"

"I'm all ears," she prompted.

"Well, we need to be able to rewind the toys, but we can't climb into the water every time to do it. And even if we could, we'd be winding constantly. We need all the toys to be wound simultaneously. I need to create a pull cord for each side of the boat," said Angus.

"Okay," said Ivy.

"But the problem is the size of the knobs," said Angus. "They are tiny. They're made small so that children can grip them easily. Even Captain Hank, as good as he is with his hands, can barely grasp the things; they're so small. So what do we have that's thin enough to wrap around the knobs, and then how do we connect that into a pull cord?"

"I don't know. But I'm waiting to hear," said Ivy.

"Rubber bands! Little ones. Absolutely tiny ones. Like the ones orthodontists use on braces," said Angus.

"Where are you going to find those?" asked Ivy. "We're on an island remember? There was a lot of garbage on the beach, but I didn't see any dental junk."

"We aren't going to find rubber bands," said Angus. "We're going to make them!"

Angus borrowed Captain Hank's knife and whittled a small driftwood stick into the approximate diameter of the wind-up toy knobs. Carefully, he dunked the stick into the bubbling glue and used the knife tip to shape the molten goo into several thin rings. He slowly rotated the stick horizontally causing the hot glue to adhere to itself without dripping off. After the glue had dried and cooled, he gently prodded it off the stick. He held the tiny "rubber" band gently between his fingers and tugged. It stretched slightly without breaking. When he let go, it returned to its original size. It took many tries, a lot of frustrated screams, and several angry stomps along the beach, but eventually Angus had perfected his technique and his supply of tiny elastic bands slowly grew.

The seagull nodded her head approvingly. "Inventor in training, indeed. Well done, Angus!"

Angus tested his idea on the captain's duck. He stretched the tiny band around the knob. It took some time but it was possible. Next, he looped a thin piece of string through the rubber band and attempted to tie a small yet sturdy knot. His fingers fumbled, and he lost the end of the string. Then he had the end of the string but couldn't quite tighten it adequately. Again and again he tried. After what felt like an eternity, he had finally tied the string to the rubber band to the toy.

"It works, but it will take us days, weeks maybe, to tie all these to a pull cord," Angus groaned.

"Probably longer," corrected the captain. "I don't think I'll be able to help you." He held out his hands to show Angus how large his fingers were.

Angus' shoulders slumped. He didn't want to wait weeks to get off this island. The Fearsome Flea and his Insect Incinerator would be long gone by then.

Ivy piped up. "Maybe I can help!"

"How are you possibly going to help? You've got two webbed feet, two wings, and a thick bill. Thanks for the offer, but I think we'll do better with fingers," said Angus.

"There's no need to be rude, Angus Clark!" scolded the seagull. "You can sit here and feel sorry for yourself for the next three weeks for all I care!" The insulted and angry Ivy flew off toward the pile of washed-up debris.

"That's some bit of animal training, there, Angus," said the captain.

Angus shoved himself to his feet and stalked off after Ivy. He found her rooting around in the refuse.

"Help me find a crate or something else we can use as a cage," she said without looking at him. "And I know I'm in the garbage so don't even think about comparing me to a rat again!"

Angus began sorting through the netting. "What are we doing this for?" he asked.

"You need to put me in a cage," said Ivy.

"What?" Angus stopped and stared at her. "Whatever for?"

"I like this body. It's fast and strong and I feel invincible. I don't want to lose it," said Ivy.

"Why would you lose it?" asked Angus.

"The seagull will fly away when I move bodies. I can't help you build the boat in this one," she said matter-of-factly. "I don't know if we're going to find anything. Maybe you should wrap me up in netting."

Angus shook his head. "Too dangerous. What if the not-you seagull tries to escape and injures its wing in the rope?"

"Good point," agreed Ivy.

"What if we drop you in Captain Hank's sack? It's dark, soft, and no holes to get stuck in," suggested Angus.

"I guess that would work," said Ivy.

"I'll go get it," offered Angus running off.

"Meet me at the forest," Ivy called after him.

When they reunited a few minutes later, Ivy explained the plan to Angus. He would put her in the sack, carry her into the forest, and sit quietly a few feet from her until she called him. He would, under no circumstances, leave her alone. The seagull would be defenseless while trapped in the sack. He did as she instructed and sat down to wait, his back resting against a tree.

Angus sat in the dim forest and listened to the soft wind play with the boughs above his head. The moss beneath his legs and bottom was soft and cozy. He began to feel drowsy. He'd not been very successful at sleeping outdoors on the beach the night before. He didn't know when exactly he dozed off, but he woke with a start to high-pitched, angry squeaking and a sharp pain in his finger. He looked at his hand and was surprised to see a little mouse standing on its hind legs squealing at him.

"I ask you to do one measly thing and you can't even stay awake long enough!" The little animal's whiskers twitched, and its front paws rested indignantly at its waist. It was all Angus could do not to laugh. The mouse saw him smile though and grew angrier still. "If you're going to make fun of me you can just sit here on this island and rot! I don't need to help you, you know!"

"Hey there, calm down Ivy!" insisted Angus. "I was just startled to see you as a field mouse, that's all."

"I'm not a field mouse! Do you see a field here? And you call yourself a scientist! I'm a shrew mouse! Get it right. Geesh! I should leave right now! Leave you to do this all yourself!" she squeaked at him.

"I'm sorry you're feeling so upset. I apologize, okay? May I pick you up or did you want to bite my finger again?" asked Angus.

"I feel so angry! Everything is irritating me right now! Your big head bothers me! My skin itches! My front tooth hurts! Stop breathing on me! I just want to …. arggg … bite something!" announced Ivy. "Let me ride on your shoulder and don't just leave that bag laying over there. You've got to protect that seagull. I'm going to want to get back in there … this shrew mouse body is awful … I want to take it off!"

"Right now?" asked Angus scrambling to his feet and hustling over to the sack twitching on the forest floor.

"Of course not! That won't help anything, you numbskull! The seagull can't help you fix the boat! You need somebody small, and fast, and wily. That's a shrew mouse."

16

Seaworthy

The three friends worked late into the night. The two humans took turns holding a torch to light their efforts. Ivy was able to work quickly in the dark. "I have terrible vision even in the daylight. I prefer to use my other senses," the shrew mouse explained.

Captain Hank glued the remaining wind-up toys to the second animal trough. Angus painstakingly wrapped a tiny elastic band around each knob. Ivy scurried from one toy to the next, lacing the thin strings through each knob and tying knots with her dexterous paws and cutting the string with her sharp teeth. Finally, Captain Hank gathered all the string ends and tied them to a rope, and then sealed the knot with the remaining glue.

When they were satisfied that the boat was completed, Angus carried the sleeping seagull and the tiny shrew mouse back to the forest. Ivy moved back into the gull's body, and the terrified shrew ran into the underbrush. Angus opened the sack to release Ivy and walked back to the beach. He and the captain fell straight to sleep. Angus must have been exhausted, because he slept soundly until Captain Hank shook him awake the next morning.

Angus pulled the woolen blanket over his head and rolled on to his side. "Leave me alone. Tired. More sleep."

The woolen blanket flew off him. "Get your lazy self up!" chided the captain. "The tide's in this morning. We need to get the boat in the water. Right now!"

Angus groaned and rubbed the sleep from his eyes. He blinked, squinting against the glare burning through the light morning fog. Captain Hank reached his large hand down and hauled Angus to his feet. He tossed Angus' pants to him, and Angus hurriedly put them on. There was no sign of Ivy yet this morning.

He stumbled along behind the energetic captain. They each grabbed a side of the boat and pushed. It jutted along toward the lapping water and they climbed in. The hard plastic was a bit uncomfortable, and Angus imagined how stiff and sore his body would feel after sitting in the boat for several hours. He opened his mouth to complain, but then he saw the tall captain in the other animal trough. He had squeezed his lanky body into the rigid plastic enclosure. His long legs were crammed tightly into the opening. His angular chin rested on his bony knees. He saw Angus looking at him and smiled jovially.

"I've sailed in worse," he grinned.

"Wait! We forgot an anchor!" said Angus.

"No need," responded the captain. "We're just going to test her seaworthiness. If she floats, we'll take her around to East Beach and tether her by the cliff. If she sinks, we'll know soon enough and haul her back up here."

A large wailing call broke through the fog, and Ivy splashed down beside them. "The boat seems to be floating."

And indeed it was.

"Let's try out the motor," suggested Angus.

"Yes. On three," agreed Captain Hank.

"One, two, three," counted Ivy.

Angus gave his rope a gentle tug. Nothing happened. The captain's side wasn't working either. Maybe he hadn't pulled hard enough?

"Count again," said the captain.

"One, two, three," said Ivy.

Angus used more force the second time. After a millisecond delay the motor sprang to life. With a quiet splashing sound reminiscent of a wood duck landing on a pond, the strange vessel began to move forward. It cut slowly, ploddingly, through the waves that were still moving toward shore.

"We'll move faster if we wait until the tide starts flowing out again," observed Angus.

"Yes, but if there's a problem it will be more difficult to get back to shore," explained the captain. "Once we're sure she works, we can wait for the outgoing tide."

"Aye, aye, Captain!" said Angus saluting like a sailor. The captain grinned appreciatively at him.

After a few short minutes the splashing stopped. Angus looked to Captain Hank and awaited orders. "Again!" announced the captain. Angus tugged the rope, and the boat began moving again. After a few more minutes the boat stopped. "That's not going to work," said the captain. "We can't just stop dead in the water. We have to pull at different times so some part of the motor is always running. You pull, I'll count to ten, and then I'll pull. That will send us forward."

"What if we want to turn?" asked Angus.

"Have you ever rowed a canoe?" asked Captain Hank.

"My parents took me a few times," said Angus.

"What did you do if you wanted to turn?"

Angus considered for a moment. "If I wanted to go left, I'd paddle on the right side. To turn right, I'd paddle on the left."

"Exactly." The captain beamed at him. "When we're facing the front, or the bow of a boat, the left of the boat is the port side. The right is called starboard. I'm sitting on the starboard side, so if we want to turn to port, I'll pull my rope. You're sitting on the port side, so you'll pull if we want to turn to starboard. Make sense?"

Angus nodded. "Can we try it?"

"Sure," agreed the captain. "Let's go forward first, and then we'll practice turning."

Angus pulled his cord, the captain pulled his, and they practiced different combinations of forward motion and turning. Ivy interrupted their exercises announcing, "I'm flying back to shore before all the food's gone."

Seagulls flocked to the beach where the receding tide had exposed a banquet of shellfish. Neither Angus nor the captain had noticed that the tide had changed. "Looks like we're on our way," said the captain.

The three friends met up again an hour later at East Beach. Captain Hank unfolded his stiff legs from the boat and climbed out in to the rocky shallows. He stretched his aching back and tight leg muscles. Angus tossed him a rope and the captain tethered the boat to some overhanging tree limbs. Angus climbed out and the two waded to shore.

A seagull was chasing the surf up and down the beach poking hopefully at broken shells and marine detritus as they washed up.

"Ivy? Is that you?" called Angus.

The seagull dropped the empty shell it was holding and squawked at him. "Yes! What took you so long?"

"We were fighting currents the entire way," explained the captain. "The island and shallow rocks create them. I expect the boat will move faster when we're farther from land."

"Well? What's the plan?" asked Ivy.

"We get in the boat and chase the Fearsome Flea," said Angus.

"Yes, obviously." The seagull rolled her eyes. "But then what? What do we do once we find it?"

Angus and the captain stared blankly at each other.

"You have got a plan, haven't you?" pressed Ivy.

They looked at her.

"I mean, you have given it a little bit of thought? You don't think we'll just arrive, ring the doorbell, and the pirates will cheer for your safe return and invite you to stay for dinner and a movie, do you?" she asked sarcastically.

"There are no movies onboard the Fearsome Flea," said Captain Hank, happy to finally be able to offer some information.

Ivy snorted.

"No projector," he added.

She glared at him.

"No videos either." His voice trailed off, and he looked humbly at his feet.

"I guess I was so focused on building a boat and getting off the island, I didn't think about what would happen next," said Angus.

The three friends stood blinking at each other.

"Well, I'm hungry." The captain broke the silence. "I'm going to start a fire and get something cooking."

"That's a start," said Ivy. "Then what?"

"If you're so smart why don't you offer a suggestion?" whined the captain. "Begging your pardon, Angus. But your pet can be truly exasperating."

"No need to apologize," Angus grinned. He wasn't an expert on seagull facial expressions but it sure looked like Ivy was scowling at being called his pet. "I agree, sometimes she is a bit annoying." Ivy squawked at him, ruffled her feathers, and flew off.

"You do know she's right though?" asked the captain once they were alone.

"Of course she is. We need a plan." Angus thought for a moment. "If you were still pirating, how would you board an enemy ship?"

"Well, I'd raise the Jolly Roger. Send warning shots over her bow. Maybe come up alongside her and sprinkle her with case shot," said the captain. "It's all based on bluster, a show of strength. You strike fear into the hearts of your enemies. Either they surrender or you board and fight. You and me and your seagull in a tiny plastic boat coated in children's toys?"

"Not exactly awe-inspiring," concluded Angus.

The captain shook his head sadly.

"You'll need to sneak on to the ship," said Ivy, who had flown up silently behind them. "Your boat has two things going for it. It's quiet, and it's small. If you arrive under cover of darkness, you can sneak aboard, find Angus' contraption-thingy, and sneak back off before the pirates even know you're there."

"That would work," said Angus. "But what about the captain? How's he going to get the Fearsome Flea back?"

Ivy rolled her eyes. "I can't think of everything! We can help him get back on his ship, but he's going to have to figure out how to get his crew to follow him again."

"And that's the hardest part," sighed the captain.

It was decided that Ivy would perform a reconnaissance mission to discover where the Fearsome Flea was. The captain and Angus sat down for a warm meal and then retired to the hut for an afternoon nap. They would set out in their small plastic boat at dusk so the pirates would not observe their slow approach.

Ivy poked Captain Hank gently awake when she returned. He tiptoed out of the hut so as not to wake Angus.

"I found them in the Sound. I'm not sure how far out. I flew there, rested my wings a while on deck, and then flew back," Ivy explained.

"We're lucky they didn't head out to sea." The captain looked at the sun's position in the sky. "You left shortly after noon. It will be dusk in another hour. You've been gone three and a half, maybe four hours. They're close, really close. It will take us longer by water. Maybe twice as long." He considered for a moment. "If we want to get there before the sun comes up, we need to leave soon. You'd better go wake Angus. I'll pack our supplies. We set sail in ten minutes."

17

Ivy Saves the Day

The dark surrounded them. The gentle splashing sound of the paddle motor was masked by the slapping waves. The boat slogged forward. It painstakingly climbed one wave and was jostled to the side by another. Sometimes a swell would lift the boat and propel it forward like a surfer riding the waves. Their progress was slow, yet steady, like the famous turtle who won the race.

Angus settled into the relaxed motion of the boat. He rested his head against the edge of the plastic trough and gazed up at the clear midnight sky. Galaxies millions of miles away glittered back at him. Ivy was nestled at his side, her head concealed beneath a protective wing. Her soft feathery body was warm against his hip.

Even though he'd had an afternoon nap, his body was heavy and tired. The gentle rocking of the boat would have put him to sleep if he hadn't had to keep pulling on the rope every few minutes. Several times, his focus drifted and he forgot to wind the motor. The boat began to list to port. Captain Hank, wide awake with discomfort in his tightly-fitting side of the boat, barked "Look sharp!"

The captain welcomed the pain in his knees and back. He had spent most of his life on the sea; it was his home, and he only felt truly alive on it. The blood coursed through his veins like hot pepper sauce. He was wide awake, his senses alert. He heard every small noise on the water. Like a nocturnal animal, he scanned the vista for movements and irregularities. Every minute that passed, every drop of water left behind in their wake, was a minute, a drop, closer to his ship. His Fearsome Flea. He was the rightful owner. It was his future, his legacy. He was honor-bound to captain her again.

And then he saw it. Instinctively, he leaned his body forward and squinted into the night. The seascape divided into two distinct fields. The silvery black waves undulated up and down, side to side. The solid black sky was broken by tiny flecks of light, the stars. Floating between those two fields was a gray vagueness. It grew larger, and the outline was clearly that of a one-masted ship. Closer and closer it came.

"Angus!" he breathed.

"Wha, wha, yes Captain. I wasn't asleep that time. Just lost track," the boy claimed.

"There she is. Do you see her?" Captain Hank pointed.

Angus was instantly wide awake. He strained forward squishing Ivy against the side of the boat.

"Ouch!" she squawked. "Get off me, you big gorilla!"

Angus wiggled to give her room, rocking the boat precariously. In their excitement, both he and the captain had forgotten to wind the motor and the boat was at the mercy of the waves.

"Pull your string," stage whispered the captain. "We don't want to capsize this thing. Not when we're almost there!"

The little black boat sprang to life. Disaster averted, Angus scrutinized the horizon. "I don't see the ship, Captain."

"She's just off our starboard side, lad." He pointed. Angus followed the direction of his finger and glimpsed a pale gray shape moving toward them. At their present course, it would completely pass them by.

"Captain, will we make it?" Angus asked.

"We need to come about and head her off before she goes past. Pull, son. Pull like crazy," answered the captain.

Angus tugged on his rope, waited a moment until he felt the motor slow down, and then pulled again before it stopped altogether. Again and again he pulled, the captain anxiously nibbling his nails beside him. One more tug and the little plastic boat would be pointed in exactly the right direction to intercept the larger vessel. Angus heard a "snap!" The rope slackened and the boat stopped, once again tossed about by the waves.

Angus gasped, not believing. The captain barked, "Pull, young lad! Pull! We're losing ground!"

"I ... I ... can't." Angus stared at the rope lying uselessly in his hands. His mind reeled. He scrawled through blueprints in his brain. How could he possibly fix this? And fix it in time? "It's broken," he gulped.

"Broken?" The captain was incredulous. "It can't be broken! We're almost there! Can you fix it?"

Angus shook his head. "No, sir. We can hope that the current takes us somewhere inhabited or someplace with enough resources to fix our boat, build another one, or catch a ride."

He slumped into the boat. He had been so sure of himself, of his invention, of the motor, he hadn't bothered to consider a back-up plan. They had packed neither oars nor sail. They had worked so hard on this boat. A little more planning and they might have succeeded. And weighing on his conscience even heavier than yet another failed invention was the realization that the Insect Incinerator was so close. His only hope to return home, but there was no way to get to it. He felt utterly defeated.

The captain growled, "No! I refuse to give up! Paddle with your hands! Paddle with all your might!" He reached his long arms into the water and dug with cupped hands. The boat didn't move. "Help me, lad! Paddle!" His voice cracked, and Angus realized that the gentlemanly captain was dangerously close to crying.

Angus reached over the side of the boat. He stretched as far as he could but was only able to touch the surface of the water with his fingertips. "I'm sorry, sir. It's no use."

The captain began to sniff, then to snort, and then he howled, "No! My ship! They've got my ship! It's not fair! I'm not going back to the island! No! You can't make me!"

Angus stared in amazement. He had never seen an adult weep and wail and throw a tantrum. Younger kids at the playground? Yes. Some of his friends during recess? Sure. Himself, on a rare occasion but only when something truly was unfair? Admittedly, from time to time, yes. But a full-grown, slightly balding, cookie-baking adult? No way. Angus had absolutely no idea how to fix this.

"Buck up, there. Um. Buddy. It will be okay," he tried, patting the captain weakly on the back. Captain Hank kept blubbering noisily. His tears spurted out like the water from the outdoor faucet that time Angus had tried to adjust the sprinkler system with a crowbar.

"Squawk! Put a plug in it, Hank! And you call yourself a sailor! A captain, even? No wonder your crew stuck you on an island. You're a pirate, for mercy's sake! Act like one!"

Captain Hank stopped mid-sob and looked at the indignant seagull. Ivy stood on the boat's gunnel, wings tucked tightly against her sides, glaring at the captain.

"It's a good thing we aren't heading straight for the Fearsome Flea. The crew could have heard you! You are lucky the wind is blowing from the other direction tonight. Is this how you lead a crew into battle?"

The captain wiped his nose and mumbled, "No."

"You are the captain of this vessel! You are the center of the ship in good times and in bad. If you lose heart what is your crew to do?" demanded Ivy.

"I don't know," sniffed the captain.

"Well, you better figure it out! We're going to need you when we get on that ship. And we're getting on that ship one way or another or my name isn't Ivy Calloway!" She squawked, and turned her attention to Angus. "Okay, science boy. Let's hear your ideas."

"Remember how hard it was to work on the motor on dry land? In the water, my fingers will numb almost immediately. And I'm not even sure the motor is fixable," protested Angus.

"So you're going to give up, like Captain Boohoo over here?" screeched Ivy.

"Come on, now. That's enough. You're being too harsh don't you think?" asked Angus, shooting a look at the red-eyed captain.

"Maybe," the peeved seagull said a bit remorsefully. "But someone's got to motivate you two pessimists! I want you on that ship as much as you want to be on that ship. I've got something pretty important riding on that contraption of yours, too, you know!" She peered at Angus. "Or did you forget that you're not the only one who wants to go home?"

Angus stared at her. In fact, he had been so preoccupied by the challenge of building the boat, and then feeling sorry for himself and missing his parents, he had neglected to think about Ivy. She had been lost far longer than he had been, and she didn't even have her own body along for comfort.

"Sorry, Ivy," he apologized shaking his head. "I don't know what to do."

"You have to think. We need you to use your brain. It's the best tool we have. We've got no raw materials. You can't get into the water. The Fearsome Flea is right there." She pointed with her bill. "We need you to be inventive without inventing something. Can you do that?"

Angus gritted his teeth and tapped his finger against his forehead. They sat in silence, the only sounds the lapping of the waves against the drifting boat and Captain Hank's sniffling.

"I've got it!" announced Angus. "But Ivy, the success of my plan depends on you."

"Just tell me what you need me to do," said Ivy.

Ivy soared above the Fearsome Flea and assessed the situation. Except for one heavy-lidded pirate at the helm the deck was empty. She landed lightly by the trapdoor, tilted her head to the side, and listened intently. Snoring rumbled below decks. Good. Most of them were asleep. Better find Maniacal Marge.

Ivy shuffled her short legs to the captain's quarters. A stream of light slipped through the gap under the door. Drat! She was still awake. Now what? Ivy pressed her head to the door. Nothing but silence met her ears. She flapped to the doorknob and poked at it. Well, that was pretty useless. She didn't have fingers and thumbs in this body. She snorted. No monkeys on board to jump into so she'd have to think of something else.

The ship took a wave and keeled slightly to starboard. The captain's door swung open smacking the distracted seagull in the chest. She grunted from the impact, quickly recovered herself, and fluttered through the opening into the room. The door clapped shut behind her and then swung open again. The latch must be broken.

Her eyes scanned the room. She squawked in alarm and flapped back in the direction from which she'd come. Marge sat at the captain's desk directly in front of the swinging door. The desk lamp shone full on her face and Ivy realized that the tyrant's eyes were closed. The ship swayed to the side, slamming the door again, and Marge slumped forward. Her head hit the surface of the desk, and she let out a large groan and began snoring.

Ivy breathed a sigh of relief and looked around the room. There must be something here she could use to hold the door shut. This bird body wasn't strong enough to drag something heavy. Marge's ink-stained fingers clutched a fountain pen. Ivy tiptoed across the surface of the desk and gripped the pen in her bill. Just then, the ship rocked, and Marge flung her hand across Ivy's feathered head. Ivy tried not to retch. The stench of fried chicken on Marge's fingers was overwhelming. Ivy scrambled away, clutching the pen, and tumbled to the floor. She dropped the pen and gagged, then took several deep breaths to clear the repulsive burned avian smell from her nasal passages.

"I hate pirates. Disgusting creatures," she muttered, picked up the pen, and escaped out the swinging door.

When she'd reached the deck again, she waited for the door to slam shut. She worked quickly, jamming the pen into the bottom hinge. She stepped back from the door and waited for the next wave. She felt the ship rock beneath her feet. This time, the captain's door stayed shut. The solution wasn't guaranteed to keep a truly maniacal Marge locked in but it should buy them some time.

Next, Ivy flew back to the helm. The pirate on duty gazed fixedly forward. His body leaned heavily on the wheel. Several times, Ivy saw him jerk his head up, blink quickly, and pinch himself. He needed a little help to fall completely asleep. Ivy smiled to herself. This was too easy.

She hovered in the shadows and threw her voice. It was a bit squeaky in this body, but it was the best she could do.

"You are getting very sleepy, very sleepy," she squawked softly. "Your eyes are heavy. You cannot keep them open any longer." She tried not to giggle as she watched the man's body relax. "You feel the need to grip the wheel. Turn the wheel to starboard. You must turn the wheel to starboard," she droned. She continued speaking in a monotone, calmly and evenly. Within minutes the Fearsome Flea was headed straight for the captain and Angus.

"You are too sleepy to stay on deck. You must retire to your cozy bunk. You are walking to the bunkroom." Ivy flapped behind the slowly moving, slumbering pirate. "You are lifting the trapdoor. You are quietly closing the trapdoor. You are going to your bunk." The door closed behind the man and Ivy listened carefully to the thump, thump, thump, as he fell down the ladder. Oh no. She strained her ears but only heard snoring. She sighed with relief. She never regretted having taught herself hypnotism.

She looked regretfully at the closed trapdoor. Too bad she couldn't prop something heavy against it. But anything she could move with her weak seagull body would be too easy for a crew of angry pirates to dislodge. Better to get on with it before any of them awoke.

She flew to the gunnel and wailed with her seagull cry. She heard a response in kind, closer than she could have hoped. Other birds would be sleeping at this time of night, so there was no confusion about who had echoed her. "Angus! Captain! Is that you?" she called.

"Just a few yards off starboard," said the captain's voice. "If you can bring her in a bit closer, I think we'll be able to reach."

Ivy made her way to the helm and leaned against the left side of the wheel with all her might. It was heavy, and she could barely get it to budge. She flew against it hard, knocking the wind out of herself. She flew against it again and felt a welt begin to swell on the side of her body. As she gathered her strength and courage to wound herself again to save her friends, she heard a 'chunk' from the hull.

She staggered to the side, and looked over the gunnel. White teeth gleamed at her from the water. Angus stood grinning in the little black boat, pulling on a rope that towed it nearer and nearer the Fearsome Flea. As the boat drew up alongside the pirate ship, he tugged hard on the rope to dislodge his screwdriver from the wood hull. The rope and tool tumbled down into the boat.

"Step back, Ivy. I don't want to hit you," he called softly.

She fluttered away quickly. The screwdriver sailed over the ship's railing with a thud. Ivy flew to the railing and pulled on the line. Once she had enough slack, she gripped the rope and wrapped it around the railing three times.

"Give it a tug," she called down.

Angus pulled several times. "Feels secure," he said. "Captain?"

The captain reached around from his side of the boat and tugged. "Should be good. You go first," he said. "If the rope doesn't hold you I'll be here to retrieve you from the water."

Ivy agreed with this suggestion. It sounded like the captain was leading again.

Angus gripped the rope. He thought back to his phys ed class, and the month Mr. Mulligan had forced them to climb rope. Even though he was a powerful swimmer, Angus had realized quickly that he had some serious upper body strength issues. It was much easier to use your arms to propel yourself through water than to climb up a vertical rope. Once Mr. Mulligan had taught him to wrap the rope around his legs and use them to grip it, he was able to inch up the rope to the ceiling.

Now he bent his head back and looked up the long expanse of rope hanging from the side of the Fearsome Flea. He took a deep breath and decided to focus on the little bit of rope directly in front of him.

This is what he had to do to get his invention back. He must climb this rope if he ever wanted to see his parents again. He clenched his teeth and began to climb. He strained and pulled. His arms drew him up and his legs scooted behind. Arms, then legs, up the rope. But the more he climbed, the more he pulled, the weaker his arms became. They were on fire. He couldn't possibly go any farther. He didn't look down. He would get vertigo and plummet to his death. He knew it. His heart pounded faster and harder, and he began gasping for air. He squeezed his eyes shut. "I can't hold on. I'm going to fall," he gasped.

"Always drama with you men," Ivy's voice declared.

It sounded close. Angus opened his eyes and looked up. One more hand and he'd be over the railing. He reached up, gave one last hard pull, and tumbled to his back on to the deck. As he lay panting on the ground, Captain Hank clambered up.

Angus sat up and was hauled to his feet and folded into a bear hug by an exuberant Captain Hank.

18

House Arrest

The Booty Poker was in lock down, and Mrs. Clark was the prison warden.

On the first day of his house arrest, BP had been forced to clean his room. Besides picking up and organizing the colorful building blocks strewn about the carpet, he'd had to alphabetize and shelve all the books standing in piles as well as sort the dirty laundry into colors and whites. Once that was done, Mrs. Clark had instructed him on proper dusting and vacumning techniques. When he'd completed his training to her satisfaction, she had made him put his newly acquired skills to use, not only in his bedroom but in the living and dining rooms as well. And then, he was expected to complete all of the classwork he was missing in school.

He'd been so tired at the end of that day that he had welcomed the soft, warm bed. He had decided to spend one more day on land before venturing back to sea.

On the second day of his internment, Mrs. Clark had taught him how to use the washing machine and dryer, and he'd been required to do all the laundry in the house while she enjoyed a slice of chocolate cake and an hour to read the latest bestselling novel. She had not trusted him to use the iron, so she had put her book down and completed the job while he started the day's schoolwork.

BP had thought about sneaking out of the house right before Mr. Clark returned from work, but the thought of wrapping himself in a clean, warm towel after climbing out of a sudsy bath caused him to linger a bit too long.

At breakfast this morning, the third day of his suspension from school, Mrs. Clark had announced that she would be teaching him to make the day's dinner. After consulting her recipes, it was decided that with her help he would prepare the family a roasted chicken served with mashed potatoes, gravy, and peas.

After some initial hesitation, BP came to like the idea. He'd never cooked anything before. He was the Fearsome Flea's powder monkey, not the galley boy. After he'd finished his schoolwork and completed the household chores to Mrs. Clark's satisfaction, she gave him an apron and told him to wash his hands.

When he returned from the bathroom, a naked, headless chicken waited for him in the kitchen sink. Under Mrs. Clark's watchful eye, BP washed and dried the bird, seasoned it, and popped it in the oven to roast. He cut up onions and carrots and put them in a pot with the chicken's giblets to make gravy.

Mrs. Clark then taught him to shell peas. He peeled open the protective casings and ejected the little green pellets with his thumb. After that, she showed him how to peel potatoes. He still hadn't found his dagger, but Mrs. Clark assured him that she had a tool specifically for the job. He perched himself on a stool at the kitchen counter and got to work. Slice after slice flew off the potatoes. Mrs. Clark cut them into bits, and BP dropped them into a pot of boiling water.

All the preparations having been completed, Mrs. Clark allowed him to take a break. BP wandered around aimlessly, unsure what to do with this newfound freedom. He pulled absently at his earlobe fingering the pierced holes. He had half a mind to steal himself some new jewelry. He glanced at Mrs. Clark bent over a sink full of dishes and thought better of it.

He wandered up to his clean and ordered bedroom. The empty book bag lay discarded by the closet door. He opened one of the bureau drawers and glanced at the freshly laundered shirts. He could pack the book bag with a change of clothes, climb out the window, and run down to the dock.

He'd be aboard the Fearsome Flea before she even knew he was gone. He leaned his elbows on the window sill and peered out at the dreary day, drizzle rolling down the glass pane. He really didn't want to go out into that weather. The scent of garlic-and-rosemary-encrusted chicken wafted into the room. He certainly didn't want to leave before he'd tasted the dinner he was helping to cook.

BP pressed his forehead against the cool window pane. He felt drowsy and content. He looked to the fluffy comforter on top of the bed. A nap would feel good right about now. He didn't remember the last time he'd been able to lie down in the middle of the day. If he tried, Maniacal Marge would be sure to wake him up with a boot kick to his ribs. But the woman downstairs was not Marge; she was his mother.

He curled up under the comforter and closed his eyes.

BP woke to the sound of Mrs. Clark's voice. "Angus. Wake up, Honey. It's time to carve the chicken." He stretched his arms and legs and yawned. He opened his eyes and saw Mrs. Clark smiling down at him.

"Come on, dear. I pulled your roast chicken out of the oven a while ago. While it rests, why don't we mash the potatoes?"

BP inhaled the delicious scents wafting from the kitchen and jumped out of bed. He felt reenergized and eager to finish making the meal. He hurried downstairs and took the potato masher from Mrs. Clark's hand. He plunged it up and down into the steaming potatoes while she drizzled cream into the pot. Once the potatoes were mashed, he drained the peas and placed them in a small serving bowl. Mrs. Clark had set the table while he napped and all that was left was to carve the chicken.

"Where's me dagger?" he asked.

"I'll carve the chicken, Angus. The electric carving knife is too dangerous for you to use," said Mr. Clark newly returned from work and hovering eagerly in the doorway.

"I'm no wee lad! I cooked the bird. Surely I can carve it, too!" insisted BP.

"I said it's too dangerous," repeated Mr. Clark forcefully.

BP scowled. He knew better than to argue with Mr. Clark when he sounded like that.

"What if we don't use the electric knife this one time?" Mrs. Clark asked gently. BP stared. What was this? Was she actually going to take his side for once? "Maybe you could teach him how to use the carving knife safely?"

Mr. Clark looked at her, considering.

"I mean, he made the entire meal. It's only right that he should carve the meat, too," she said. "But safely. With your help."

Mr. Clark nodded. "Okay." He reached to the knife block and cautiously extracted a large knife. He set it on the counter and turned to BP. "Now, the way you hold this is ..."

BP's eyes gleamed, and he grabbed the knife in his right hand. He whipped it through the air, wielding it like a sword. He had trained extensively with Shep on fencing techniques. Shep insisted that he be able to adequately handle blades and defend himself before he could participate in battles.

"Angus! Be careful!" shrieked Mrs. Clark.

Under their astonished eyes, BP proficiently separated the chicken's wings and legs from its body and rapidly sliced the chicken into paper thin strips. He placed the knife beside the magnificently carved chicken with a flourish and stepped back beaming at the Clarks.

"Where did you learn to do that?" stammered Mr. Clark.

Mrs. Clark shook her head and carried the platter to the dining table. She set it down and turned back to the kitchen to fetch the bowl of peas. BP grabbed the mashed potatoes, and Mr. Clark reached for the gravy.

Sir Schnortle sat beside his bowl of cat kibble and watched the family assemble the meal. The gorgeous scent of roasted dead bird tickled his nostrils. On the table, he watched gentle juices flow down the sides of the succulent meat. He looked down at his unappetizing, dry, diet cat food.

BP watched horror-struck as his nemesis jumped to the table, sat on top of the chicken platter, and then ran off with a chicken wing clutched between his jaws.

"I'll get ye fer this, ye treacherous villain!" BP yelled. He thrust the bowl of mashed potatoes into Mrs. Clark's hand and raced off after the fleeing feline.

Sir Schnortle moved surprisingly fast despite his above-average girth. He saw a gap under the living room sofa and scurried toward it. He extended his claws and grabbed the carpet, trying to tow himself under. His swollen stomach slowed him down just enough for BP to reach him before he'd managed to scoot both back legs through the opening.

BP grabbed the cat's back leg to prevent further forward movement and gripped the animal's bloated midsection. He pulled, and the body of the heavy cat began moving back out from under the sofa. BP heard the low throated growls muffled by the chicken flesh still clamped in the greedy cat's jaws.

"Ouch! Ye stabbed me!" shouted a shocked BP.

He hauled out the fat cat, who only now dropped the chicken wing so he could spit and hiss at the young pirate. He swiped his outstretched claws at BP's face, but BP was beginning to better understand this animal, and he dodged its swipes.

"Ye are a wicked scallywag! No one hornswaggles The Booty Poker, be he the fiercest pirate on all the seas!" pronounced BP.

Mrs. Clark's calm voice broke through his oaths. "Angus, put Sir Schnortle down."

"But he ruined me dinner! I worked so hard to prepare it," blustered BP.

"I know dear. But he's just an animal and doesn't know any better. We'll order a pizza or something," she soothed.

"But I don't want a pizza! I want me chicken!" said BP.

"I know, Honey. I'm upset too. But you need to put him down," she insisted.

BP looked at Mrs. Clark and glowered at the hissing Sir Schnortle. "Don't think this is over, ye bilge rat!" He released the cat.

Sir Schnortle ran to the hallway, then turned around, raised his hackles, glared at BP, and let out one last hiss. It didn't appear that he was done with the battle yet either.

19

The Hold

Captain Hank walked slowly across the deck. He gazed around in wonder, his face glowing. He walked to the helm and stroked the wheel lovingly, like a mother smoothing the hair from a child's forehead. Tears welled in his eyes. He was home.

Angus and Ivy watched him silently for a moment.

"We've got to get moving, Angus," whispered the seagull. "The pirates are asleep now but dawn is approaching."

Angus glanced at the lightening sky and knew she was right.

"We have to find my Insect Incinerator. Where do we begin?" he thought out loud. "Where do pirates keep their treasure? Ivy, you used to live on board. Where did the crew stash their loot after a battle?"

"I didn't live here that long," Ivy began. "I only witnessed a few attacks. Both times, Marge tallied up the items and then personally carried them down those stairs."

"When I was captain, I recorded the items we had obtained in my log book. The treasure was then stored in the hold, below decks," the captain chimed in. "I can't imagine things have changed that much while that usurper has been running things."

Angus walked to the trap door. "Is there another way to get down there?" he asked.

"No," Ivy and Captain Hank said in unison.

"That means," Angus began, the blood leaching out of his face as he realized just what that did mean.

"You have to walk through the bunkroom to get to the hold," finished Ivy.

"Past all those sleeping pirates. In the dark. Without waking them," gulped Angus.

"And you'd better do it soon," added Ivy. The first rays of sun were peeking over the horizon.

The captain handed him a book of matches. "The hold is toward the bow of the ship. Pass all the bunks, and the door is there. Maniacal Marge probably has the key. I don't know how you'll unlock the door."

Angus tugged on his trusty screwdriver hanging around his neck. "I should be able to jimmy open the lock."

The captain nodded. "Yes, that should work."

Angus looked down at his too-big pink rhinestone sneakers. They protected his feet but he was clumsy in them. He couldn't risk tripping on them down below. He unlaced them and handed them wordlessly to the captain. He touched the screwdriver around his neck for good luck, grazed the top of Ivy's feathery head lightly with a finger, and then reached down and hauled up the trap door. After one last look at Ivy, he crept down the ladder.

When his bare feet left the last rung and touched the floor, Angus tried not to imagine what exactly made it so sticky. He heard the gentle breathing, snoring, and the occasional snort of sleeping men. The bunkroom was black as the wood he'd charred in the campfire. He squeezed his eyes shut and pressed his palms against the lids. When he opened them again, he could almost make out the fuzzy outline of the bunks. He scanned the floor ahead of him, and saw some gray shapes there, too. Perhaps some of the crew had fallen asleep on the floor.

He pressed his back to the hull and tiptoed softly toward the bow, carefully avoiding those unlucky few pirates. When he could go no further, he felt the wall in front of him. The fingers of his right hand touched a cold metal ring. He slid them a bit lower and felt the indentation of what he assumed was the keyhole. It was a large opening, and he prodded it with his index finger. He could feel a small piece of metal hanging down. If he could push it upward with his screwdriver, he could probably gain entrance to the hold.

He replaced his right hand with his left and kept one finger in the keyhole. If he disconnected his hand from the door, it might take him several precious minutes to find the hole again in the dark. With his right hand, he removed the screwdriver from around his neck. He poked it into the hole as far as it would go and pushed steadily upward. With a "click", the lock disengaged.

Angus pushed on the unlocked door, but it was jammed. He glanced warily over his shoulder. All the men slept. He drew a deep breath for courage and threw his weight into his right shoulder. It bounced painfully off the door. He bit his lip so as not to cry out and grabbed his injured shoulder with his left hand. His screwdriver clattered to the floor. He bent down to quickly retrieve it, and the door moved slightly outward. So that was it! The door opened toward the bunkroom, not into the hold.

With another quick look at the slumbering crew, Angus darted into the room. He closed the door carefully behind him and threaded his screwdriver through the metal ring on the inside of the door turning it sideways and lodging it against the door jamb. It would take a bit of effort for someone to open the door from the outside.

He stuck his hand into his jean pocket and drew out the book of matches. He struck one, and it ignited with a tiny burst of sulfur. The few inches directly in front of his face were illuminated. He checked the walls and noted an oil lantern installed near the door. The tiny flame scorched his finger, and he blew it out. He struck another match and lit the oil lamp. The wick caught flame, and a warm glow grew and grew casting light into the hold. Angus quickly lit a matching lantern on the opposite wall. Except for the deepest corners at the far side of the bow, Angus could now see the contents of the hold.

What he saw amazed him. Where he expected casks of gold and chests of jewels, piles of sacks greeted his eyes. He scanned the floor. They looked to be sacks of flour. He bent down and peered at the writing on one: "Sodium Bicarbonate." He read one label after another. They were all baking soda! He crawled into the corners of the bow and there was more of the same. Except for the occasional bag of ill-smelling and rotting produce there was nothing down here except baking soda.

Angus slumped on to the nearest sack. What kind of lame pirate ship was this? He wasn't entirely certain how this world worked, but in his world, or at least in the books and movies of his world, pirates attacked merchant ships for valuable treasure.

Focus, focus, he thought. He wasn't down here for jewels. He was after the Insect Incinerator. It didn't matter to him that the crew of the Fearsome Flea had no piles of money down here. Clearly, they hadn't stashed his Incinerator down here either. He was going to have to tiptoe through the bunkroom again and tell Ivy they were just as stuck now as they had been before on the island.

He stood and drew a deep breath. Courage. He blew out both lanterns and slipped the screwdriver from the door. He wrapped the string of his screwdriver around his wrist and wielded the tool like a knife. It was his only protection if one of the pirates awoke.

He closed his eyes and waited for them to adjust to the darkness. He put his ear to the keyhole and listened. He didn't hear any voices and hoped the crew was still asleep. Slowly, carefully, he pushed open the door and slipped out. Back pressed against the wall, he made his way to the ladder. He picked up one foot and silently set it down. Inch by inch, he was creeping past the snoozing crew. He couldn't wait to get out of this smelly room, breathe some fresh sea air, and wash the stickiness from his feet. He placed his foot on the ground and stumbled over a body. He grabbed the wall and righted himself, but it was too late.

"Watch where ye're walkin', matey," growled a voice, and a hand clamped around his bare ankle.

What were the odds that this pirate would let him go, not awaken the others, that Angus could still find the Insect Incinerator and escape?

"Keep it down! Some of us are gettin' our forty winks," grumbled another.

"Aw, great. Now I need to pee," whined a third.

Angus tugged his leg free and scurried to the ladder. His screwdriver clanked against the rungs as he grabbed them and climbed up. He reached the trap door as the room below him launched into drowsy life. Someone lit a lantern in the bunkroom, and Angus pushed against the door and scrambled on to the deck.

"Well?" Ivy perched on the gunnel, watching him. "Did you find it?"

"No. It's not down there," gasped Angus. "And we have bigger problems now. The crew is waking up."

"What are we going to do? They'll kill you for sure this time if they find you," said Ivy.

"I'll get back into the little boat. Maybe find a way to coast along behind them until I think of something." Angus peered over the side, but the boat was nowhere in sight. "Where is it?" He was beginning to feel panicky. "Captain?"

Captain Hank was at the wheel, steering the ship. He looked unconcernedly at Angus. "What's that, lad?"

"The boat. Our little motor boat. Where is it?" Angus asked frantically.

"Hmmm?" asked the captain.

"The crew is awake! I need to get off the Fearsome Flea! Where's our boat?"

The captain looked puzzled.

"You know, the boat we built when we were living on the island? You did tie it up before you climbed onboard, didn't you?" asked Angus.

"Well," drawled the captain. "About that ..."

"You didn't tie it up?" demanded Angus. "You forgot?"

The captain shrugged and returned his attention to navigating the Fearsome Flea.

"What were you thinking?" Angus whipped his head around frantically looking for a place to hide.

"Well, if ye're not steerin' the bucket, who is? Ye're lucky we didn't capsize in the night!" Angry voices emanated from the bunkroom. Heavy footsteps were on the stairs and the trapdoor was being pushed open.

"Last thing I remember, I was at the wheel. Don't know how I landed down here," complained a second voice.

"Ye always were a good-fer-nuthin' layabout! Ye could have killed us all!" said the first voice.

"Them's fightin' words! I'll have me due!" squabbled the second voice.

Two arguing crew members emerged from below decks. Angus stood frozen in place, mouth hanging open.

"Hide! Hide!" hissed the seagull, but it was too late. One of the pirates stopped mid-oath.

"Well lookee here. Who's come a-callin' but our former powder monkey," grinned the pirate, none other but Baldy, the one who had captured Angus the last time.

The other pirate turned around, startled. It was Shep, no longer wearing the bad-smelling red shirt.

"What a surprise," he said, shooting a sideways glance at Baldy.

"Well, well, well. Looks like our little cannon boy survived his fall from grace, don't it?" sneered Baldy. "Wonder how that happened? Maybe we oughta try again, only this time I'll walk 'im down the plank, eh?"

His terrified eyes glued to Baldy's malevolent ones, Angus backed away slowly. The entire crew was slowly spilling out of the bunkroom. Angus watched their heads appearing one after another in the deck. It reminded him of the overflowing toilet that time he flushed five dinosaur hatching eggs. But instead of colorful stegosaurus and brachiosaurus toys floating to the surface, menacing pirates surrounded him on all sides.

Angus clutched the screwdriver tightly and yelled, "Keep your distance! I have a sharp tool, and I'm not afraid to use it!"

Hearty laughter exploded around him.

"Ah, look at the wee lad!"

"Fondly it is I remember me first tool!"

"He's gonna ward us all off with a screwdriver!"

Angus felt a hand grab his elbow, and he wheeled around jabbing frantically.

"Ouch! Watch it, BP! You almost stabbed out me good eye!" Billy Roberts dodged out of range of Angus' screwdriver, and readjusted his eye patch. "Now hold up, ye scallywags!" he called to the crew. "Our old friend BP has shown plenty of pluck. First, he survived yon dip in the drink. That deserves respect, don't it? And he stowed aboard our great ship under all our noses. He's a sneaky one is our

Booty Poker. Me thinks he's a fine addition to our fearsome crew."

Many of the pirates surrounding Angus and Billy nodded their heads in agreement. There was much grumbling and chuckling among the crew. One voice called from the back, "I'll bet Marge'll have somethin' to say about that."

"The mangy wench will have to answer to me!" roared a voice from the riggings.

All eyes turned upward. Down to the deck leapt Captain Hank, a brown leather three-point hat atop his head. He landed lightly beside Angus and Billy and brandished a jewel-encrusted sword. Disbelieving gasps escaped the crew.

"Shiver me timbers! It's the cap'n!"

"But, he's dead! I saw his lifeless body with me own eyes!"

"A ghost walks among us!"

"Run fer yer lives! He'll kill us all!"

Chaos reigned aboard the Fearsome Flea. Burly pirates tripped over themselves trying to escape the captain. Scrawny, half-dressed pirates scrambled into the riggings. Several even jumped overboard.

One-Eyed Billy tugged desperately on Angus' arm. "Quick! Get away! Everyone knows sailors that return from Davey Jones' locker devour the bodies of the living!"

Only Shep stood his ground, alone and unafraid. He solemnly saluted the captain and said, "Welcome home, Cap'n."

"Thank you, sailor. I hereby appoint you my new quartermaster. From the looks of this vessel, we have some work to do. Let's start by throwing out the trash."

"Aye, aye, Cap'n," grinned the sturdy pirate. "I believe she's still in her quarters."

20

The Pirate's Booty

Ivy approached Angus, who was leaning over the
ship's railing helping One-Eyed Billy tow a
shivering, bedraggled pirate to safety.

"That was weird," she observed.

"I know. I didn't realize pirates were so
unscientific," said Angus.

"Superstitious," corrected Ivy. "Why did they all
think the captain was dead?"

Angus remembered what Captain Hank had told
him when they were marooned together. "I think
One-Eyed Billy tranquilized him with chamomile
tea. Maybe they thought he was dead when he was
only asleep."

"Pirates are so superstitious," said Ivy.

"Unscientific," corrected Angus.

The seagull flew off in search of the captain.

She found him with Shep standing outside the captain's quarters. The closed door shuddered as heavy fists pounded from the inside.

"Release me, you scurvy knaves! I'll keelhaul whoever's responsible fer this!" Marge yelled from within.

"We don't know how to open the door, Marge. She's stuck, she is," called Shep.

"Well take an ax to it you bilge rat! Have I got to do everthin' meself?" she bellowed back.

Ivy fluttered to the deck and squawked to attract attention. She pointed her bill at the pen jamming the door's hinge.

"Well, lookee here," said Shep bending over. "Yon gull is tellin' us somethin'."

"That's no gull. That's Ivy," responded Captain Hank. "That's Angus' pet. For some reason, he calls them all Ivy."

"Who's Angus?" asked Shep pulling the pen from the door hinge. The door banged open smashing the thickset pirate in the face.

"Who's bloody idea was it to lock me in me quarters?" spat Maniacal Marge as she emerged from the room, dreadlocks hanging down into her face. She stopped when she caught sight of Captain Hank. "Look who's decided to set foot on me ship," she jeered. "Old fancypants hisself. What, ain't we keeping the Flea clean enough for ye?"

"As a matter of fact, the deplorable condition of this ship is an outrage, both to me and to my mother's memory," the captain said quietly. His eyes blazed and he pointed his sword at Marge's throat. "And in truth, we both know whose ship this is."

He withdrew his sword and stepped back, allowing Marge to exit the cabin. "Despite your behavior and demeanor, you are a lady, and I cannot, in good conscience, battle you."

"Yer mistake," snarled Marge and she lunged at him with her dagger.

Captain Hank dodged away, but the point of Marge's dagger had grazed his cheek and blood flowed freely. The captain's hand flew to his injury, and his face contorted into a grimace of pain and fury. He held his sword down at his side and backed away from Marge dodging each thrust with agility.

"Get her, Cap'n!" called Shep. "Fight!"

The captain shook his head. "She may deserve it, and I am more furious than I've ever been, but my dear departed mother, God rest her soul, raised me to be respectful to women."

"She's not a woman. She's a monster!" called Ivy.

"Coward!" chortled Marge. "That's why your crew didn't follow ye! Ye're not a real pirate!"

"Not true," called Billy resting against the ship's hull after having pulled five men to safety. "I jist didn't wanna clean the head nomore."

"Marge promised us untold riches," called a toothless pirate. "Didn't get those, did we?"

"Lucky to have a bite to eat of an evenin'," snorted a bone-thin pirate.

"She don't honor the pirate's code," yelped a scrawny peg-legged pirate.

"The ship's a cesspool. I can't live in this filth no more," grumbled a white-haired pirate.

"When ye stop to think about it, things weren't so bad when Cap'n was in charge, were they?" suggested Shep.

"Quiet! All of ye! Ungrateful wretches!" roared Marge. "I'll get ye all! First, I'll kill this coward of a cap'n once and fer all!"

"Not if I can help it," Angus sang out, as he plunged his screwdriver into Marge's posterior.

Marge lay moaning on a mattress across the Fearsome Flea's deck, a white bandage wrapped around her rear-end. Her hands and feet were tied behind her back. "I'll get ye, ye filthy powder monkey!" she howled. "And ye, too, Shep! Ye're a traitor, and no mistake."

One-Eyed Billy watched her wordlessly as he peeled off a sweaty gray sock. "Oh Marge, put a sock in it," he said with a twinkle in his eye and stuffed it into her mouth. She gagged and spat but was unable to speak another word.

"What's the plan now, Captain?" asked Angus.

Captain Hank stood at the ship's wheel and focused on the horizon. "We're heading in to port and turning Marge in to the police. I will testify to her theft of my ship. I've spoken to several members of the crew, and they claim she sold much of the treasure they stole. I've sent Shep to the hold to tally the remaining items. The crew will probably have to do community service to pay for their crimes. They'll have plenty of time on land. We have to put the Flea in dry dock to repair her. And I plan to pick up where I left off, marketing my Captain's Cleanser."

Angus gazed out sadly at the waves.

"What about Angus?" squawked Ivy.

"Well, he'll help me, I hope." The captain gazed down at him. "You know that you're welcome to live here as long as you like. Those inventions of yours would be a great addition to my business."

"Thanks," Angus muttered twirling his screwdriver between his fingers.

"No!" argued Ivy. "That's not right! He helped you get your ship back. You have to help him get home!"

"Get home?" asked the uncomprehending captain. "I told you, I'm bringing the Flea into dock. Of course, you can go home anytime you like."

"Squawk!" Ivy flapped her wings angrily. "He needs his machine! He can't go home without it! You need to help him find it!"

The captain considered Angus for a moment. "What do you mean you didn't find your machine? It wasn't in the hold?"

"No," mumbled Angus.

"Well, what did you find?" prompted the captain.

At that moment, Shep strode purposefully across the deck. "Captain!" he saluted.

"Yes, Quartermaster?"

"I've just been to the hold, Cap'n. There ain't no booty."

A collective gasp was heard across deck.

"How is that possible?" asked one pirate.

"Where's all the loot we stole?" said another.

"Marge ain't allowed any of us into the hold since we mutinied. We all thought she was hoardin' the plunder," said Shep.

"Take the wheel," the captain ordered a sailor. "Come with me." He waved at Shep and Angus to follow him and set off in the direction of the captain's quarters.

Angus looked over the captain's shoulder at Marge's account books strewn across the desk. Smudged fingerprints and inkblots stained the pages. Stick figure drawings with eye patches, swords, and pirate hats decorated the empty pages. Captain Hank thumbed through page after page. They were all the same. Neither letters nor numbers appeared in the book.

"What's the meanin' of this?" gasped Shep.

"Looks like Marge hasn't been keeping records," said Captain Hank. He turned on his heel and marched out of the cabin, Shep right behind him.

Angus watched them go and then began looking through the desk's drawers. He pulled books out of the short shelves built into the wall. He peered under the bed and tossed the bedclothes. He tore the cabin apart looking for his Insect Incinerator, but it was nowhere to be found. Shoulders sagging hopelessly, Angus left the room.

"What do ye mean, ye don't need no accounts?" demanded Shep. The sock had been removed from

Marge's mouth and a group of pirates hovered over her.

"Jist what I said. I'm a pirate, not a bloody banker!" shouted an irate Marge.

"But surely ye have our loot!" pleaded Baldy.

"I sold it fer food. Or did ye want ta starve?" said Marge.

"But we ain't had a decent meal fer weeks," argued Shep. "Surely, our plunder was worth more than that measly amount!"

"Ye do know what it was worth, don't ye?" asked another pirate.

Marge glared at them but said nothing.

Angus couldn't help himself. "Give her a pen. I want to see her write the number five." Marge shook her head. "How about four? Three? Can you write me a one?" Marge said nothing. "Come on, Marge," urged Angus. "Any number will do. Write!"

The pirates liked the sound of this. A chant started, "Write! Write! Write!"

Marge let out an earsplitting yell. "QUIET!" As one, the pirates stopped chanting.

"Tell them, Marge," said Angus. "Tell them you can't write numbers. You can't add. You can't subtract. You don't know how much money you had or what your treasure was worth. When it was time to sell it, did you even know how to count the money?"

Marge gave him a sullen look.

"You can rob all the innocent people you want, but if you can't understand even basic math they can rob you right back," concluded Angus.

Marge growled at him, opened her mouth, and let out a string of oaths. One-Eyed Billy stuffed the sock back into her mouth.

"She can't count?"

"Whose idea was it to make her the boss?"

"I knew somethin' was fishy."

The pirates stood around, arguing with each other.

Ivy sidled over to Angus. "How'd you know Marge couldn't do arithmetic?" she asked.

"Just a guess. I remembered how you said I was a different version of myself in each of the worlds. BP's a buffoon in this one." He looked at her. "In my world, there's a woman who looks a lot like Marge. I call her Ms. Evergood, and she's my math teacher."

The seagull nodded. "Ironic."

Angus shrugged. "It would be funny if I didn't fear she'd sold my Insect Incinerator for apples."

"Ah come on bucko, it's not so bad as all that," said One-Eyed Billy clapping his hand on Angus' shoulder.

"Actually Billy, it is. I need to get back to my parents. And I can't get there without ..." Angus stopped mid-sentence and stared at Billy's pants. A mustard yellow tool belt wrapped around his hips. He pointed a shaking finger. "Hey, where'd you get that?"

The one-eyed pirate glanced down at the toolbelt. "Easy. I ran a rig on old Marge over there." His cheek crinkled as he winked his eye. "She never was a worthy opponent."

"What do you mean? I don't understand," asked Angus.

"Come on, I'll show ye," said Billy heading for the bow. The two boys walked to the cannon. "Help me push," said Billy leaning into a crate of case shot. "Put yer back into it."

Angus grabbed a corner of the heavy crate, and he and Billy shoved it along the deck. "Good enough," said the patched boy. He pulled a hammer from the tool belt. "This should do the trick."

He worked the claw into a gap between two decking planks and pulled up. One of the planks was dislodged. He took it in his fingers and removed it from the deck revealing a deep cavity beneath.

Angus stared. "Aw, shut yer mouth, BP. Yer gonna catch flies," chuckled Billy. "Take a look." Angus peered down into the hole. The morning sunlight sparkled off of whatever was inside. He reached his hand into the cavern and pulled out a handful of coins and jewels. "Wow!" he breathed.

"Someone had to watch out fer the crew. I set aside what I could and snuck the rest out of Marge's cabin whenever I had the chance. Easy enough to hide it. No one wants cannon duty. After you walked the plank, no one dared come up here," explained Billy.

Angus' heart began to race. Billy had the pirate booty. Billy had the tool belt. Was it possible? Had he swiped the Incinerator before Marge could sell it? Eyes round as Spanish doubloons, Angus asked, "Would you happen to have the other thing, my machine? The one Marge stole from me the day I arrived, I mean, the day of the battle, when the cannon blew through the ship. The day I walked the plank."

Billy stood and reached into the nose of the cannon. "Are ye talkin' about this gadget?" he asked and pulled out Angus' Insect Incinerator. "Wasn't sure what it was. Figured it was worth somethin'." Angus snatched the refurbished barcode scanner from the pirate's hand and examined it. It looked in good shape, but it had been at the bow of the ship for days. The salt spray could have damaged the electronic components. He regarded One-Eyed Billy for a moment, and then he embraced the surprised pirate.

"You don't know what this means to me. Thanks, Billy! You are a good and true friend." A worried look crossed his face. "I hope it still works." He pointed at the tool belt. "Would you mind?" he asked.

"I never could hornswaggle a mate," sighed Billy unfastening the belt and handing it to Angus.

21

At the Pier

Saturday morning came, and Mrs. Clark announced that The Booty Poker was released from house arrest. She even handed him two five dollar bills.

"Why don't you get out of the house for a while? Go see if Billy's around and get an ice cream or something," she said.

He stared at the money in her hand and grabbed it before she changed her mind.

"Just a minute, Angus." She took his wrist, and forced him to look at her. "What you did at school this week was unacceptable. I never want a call like that from Mrs. Quigley again. Understood?"

BP nodded. "Yes, ma'am."

"Use that big brain of yours." She tapped his head. "Think first, okay? Now, go."

BP ran gleefully to his room, eager to finally get back to the Fearsome Flea. He pulled on a pair of blue jeans, a t-shirt, and a sweater. He packed a change of clothes into the book bag and stuffed the money into his pocket. He looked around the room one last time and realized he'd forgotten to make the bed. He fluffed the pillows, neatly arranged the comforter, and then threw the bag over his shoulder and raced down the stairs.

He hurried into the kitchen and grabbed Mrs. Clark around the middle.

"What? What are you doing Angus?" She laughed, pleasantly surprised by the affection. He'd never been a boy for cuddles and kisses.

"Jist wanted to say thanks fer everthin'. Ye're a grand lady, and I willna forget ye," he said as he hugged her.

"Well, Angus, I sure hope not! I am your mother after all!" She hugged him back and kissed the top of his cowlicky head. "Now, go have some fun! Before I wonder who you are and what you've done with my son!"

He released her and ran to the doorway where he'd left his sneakers. During his stay with the Clarks, he'd decided that he liked his feet to be clean and warm. He wedged his left foot into a sneaker without untying it first. He picked up the right sneaker and pushed his foot into it. He felt something warm, soft, and wet ooze through his sock.

"What the?" he mumbled to himself, and pulled the shoe off. A brown smudge was pressed to the bottom of his sock, and an acrid smell struck his nose. He peered into the sneaker and saw a small, squashed, stinky log.

"Black hearted fiend!" he roared.

Sir Schnortle had pooped in his shoe.

After scrubbing his foot, changing his socks, and grabbing a clean pair of shoes, BP gave Mrs. Clark another tight hug and set off for the port. The Clark home was two miles directly uphill from the harbor. BP alternately walked and ran down the steep streets until he reached the shore. From there, he kept the water on his right side as he jogged along the sidewalks to the dock.

He passed joggers, dog-walkers, and children riding bicycles. He was surprised to see so many landlubbers this close to the harbor. This area tended to be very unsafe what with all the roving pirates and bands of pickpockets. He grew increasingly amazed when he realized that the seaside shanties had been rebuilt and were now shining apartments and condominiums.

As he neared the harbor, he was astounded to see the clothing boutiques and expensive restaurants. Shiny cars promenaded slowly down the street, their drivers looking for parking spots. He watched a man and woman push some buttons on a machine at a corner building. His jaw dropped when the machine discharged money. He waited for them to leave, looked around to be sure no one was watching him, and hurried over to the machine. But it was no use. No matter which buttons he pushed, no money appeared. He gave up and moved on down the street.

He turned a corner and hurried to the dock. He scanned the horizon but didn't see the skull and crossbones anywhere. He slapped himself on the forehead. Of course! What was he thinking of? Maniacal Marge wouldn't be flying the Jolly Roger while they were in port. That would alert the police that a crew of pirates roamed among them. He'd have to search a little harder. The Fearsome Flea was probably camouflaged.

He prowled one wooden pier after another. He saw motor boats with one and two motors. Inner tubes and skis rested inside. He counted a dozen varieties of sailboats, from small dinghies to J boats, and several cutters. Large and small kayaks were tied to the piers and even one or two canoes. He saw a fireboat and hid his face behind his hand as he passed a police boat. BP scurried from pier to pier, but nowhere did he see the familiar face of a crew member or the welcome sight of the Fearsome Flea.

He wandered up and down the harbor, peering across the water, wondering whether the Fearsome Flea had just set sail. He fingered the money in his pocket. If he'd just missed her, he might be able to encourage a sailor to transport him. Would ten dollars be enough?

A white-haired man sat on a bench by the piers looking through a pair of binoculars. BP hurried over to him.

"Ahoy, matey!" said BP.

The old man turned his gaze to BP and lowered his binoculars.

"Did you say something, son?" he asked loudly.

"Aye. What sees ye through yer spyglass?" asked BP.

"Pardon me? My hearing's not as good as it once was," shouted the old gentleman reaching his pinkie finger into a hairy ear. He wiggled it around a bit, pulled it out, and inspected the tip of his finger.

"I'm looking fer me hearties. Old One-Eyed Billy's run a rig on me and marooned me. Can I look through yer spyglass?" BP shouted back.

"Talk into my good ear," yelled the old man pointing to his right ear.

BP leaned down and yelled into the man's ear. "See ye a sail over yonder?"

"Sally sells seashells? What are you talking about son?" the deaf man cried.

"Can I look through yer spyglass?" shouted BP.

"You may not loot my pie grass! What is pie grass anyway?" yelled the befuddled old man.

"Not pie grass! Spyglass!" shouted BP.

"Don't shout at me! Is that how your mother raised you? To yell at your elders?" shouted the man.

"Beg pardon, Sir. I'm marooned and lookin' fer me pirate ship," mumbled BP.

"Oh, your pirate ship. Why didn't you say so? I was a pirate in my youth. Haven't seen a Jolly Roger all day," said the old man. He winked at BP and creakily stood. "Now, if you'll excuse me, I'm late for a sword duel."

BP watched the elderly man shamble off. It seemed he had missed the Fearsome Flea. But instead of desperation and disappointment, BP felt a sense of relief. He thought about his warm bed and full stomach. He thought about Mr. Clark, and Mrs. Clark, and even that wretch Sir Schnortle. It wasn't entirely awful to have to live by the family rules. Not when there were chocolate cake and hot baths at the end of the day.

Maybe he wouldn't go back to the Fearsome Flea after all. Maybe he'd stay on land for a while. Get to know the Clarks again. Get to know his parents again.

His mind made up, BP clambered to his feet. He must have stood too quickly, because his head began to spin. He fell back to the bench, grabbed his head, and blacked out.

22

The Bucket

Angus retreated to the captain's quarters to inspect the Insect Incinerator. Ivy oversaw the operation from a safe distance. Angus was still unsure how he had propelled himself into this dimension. She didn't trust that he wouldn't make the same mistake again, this time at her expense.

Hidden behind a chest, she shouted out what she thought were helpful suggestions. "Are you sure the red wire goes there? Wouldn't the green one look better next to the yellow one? What if you remove that doohickey from the other thingamabob?"

Angus didn't hear her. Ivy's squeaky words floated around his head. They never made their way into his ear canal. He focused all of his attention on his beloved invention.

Despite the time it had spent rolling around inside the cannon, the Insect Incinerator was not damaged. Angus reconnected the colored wires and tightened some tiny screws. He peered into the component case and noticed a whitish film. He pulled a cotton swab from his tool belt and cleaned the inside of the case. He blew on the tip of the swab, dispersing a fine white powder into the air. The case was now clean, and he closed it and retightened the screws on the back.

He looked around the cabin. "I need to test it on something."

Ivy squawked and fluttered farther away.

"Not on you, silly! Let's find something useless that no one will miss. Any ideas?" said Angus.

"How about Marge?" suggested Ivy.

Angus considered this solemnly and then shook his head. "No. We don't want to dump her on an unsuspecting dimension. Best to leave her here." He thought a moment. "I might have just the thing!" He swung open the cabin door and called to Captain Hank. "Permission to enter the hold, sir?"

"Permission granted," beamed the blissful sailor standing at the helm. "What for? There's nothing down there but my baking soda and some rotten cabbage."

"I want to test my invention, Captain. If it works, the crew won't need to clear out the vegetables by hand," said Angus.

"Ye've got me marker if ye can do that!" said Shep, who was organizing the crew to perform some much overdo ship scrubbing.

Ivy and Angus sidestepped a bucket, a mop, and a deck-swabbing sailor, and went below decks. One sailor was stripping rancid sheets off the bunks while another scrubbed the floor with a thick, white substance. "Captain's Cleanser?" asked Angus. The sailor nodded and continued his work.

The door to the hold was propped open. Shep had ordered the molding produce to be piled into one corner for quick removal when the ship docked. The sacks of sodium bicarbonate were stacked neatly to the ceiling nearer the bow. The seagull wedged her body behind the bags and peeked around the corner.

"I'm ready," she called.

"Here goes nothing," said Angus. He pointed the Insect Incinerator at the vegetable pile and pulled the trigger. Nothing happened. Angus dropped his arm to his side, and he bowed his head to his chest. "I was afraid of that."

"Is it broken?" asked Ivy venturing warily from her hiding place.

"I dropped it at home, and it stopped working," Angus said gloomily.

"But it must have been working, or you wouldn't have crossed dimensions," insisted Ivy.

"That's true," admitted Angus. "It stopped working and I brought it into my lab."

"Okay. Let's think this through. Try to remember everything that happened from the time you dropped your invention to landing on the Fearsome Flea. What did you do when you came into your lab?" asked Ivy.

"I opened up the machine and fiddled with some wires," began Angus.

"Do the wires look the same way they did the day you traveled?" interrupted Ivy.

"Yes. I checked them in the Captain's cabin," said Angus.

"Good. Then what did you do in your home lab?" asked Ivy.

Angus wrinkled his brow and tried to remember. It was so long ago. "My mom came in."

"And?" pressed Ivy.

"She told me to clean up my lab before my dad came home from work," answered Angus.

"And did you?" asked Ivy.

"What difference does that make?" asked Angus.

"I don't know. Maybe it doesn't. But maybe it does," said Ivy. "Well? Did you clean up your lab?"

"No," said Angus.

"Oh," said Ivy.

Angus' face brightened as he remembered. "But some of the cleaner fell into the Insect Incinerator." That must have been the white film he had cleaned out with the swab!

"What kind of cleaner was it?" pressed Ivy.

Angus looked around the hold and a slow grin spread over his face. "It was a box of baking soda."

Ivy let out a large wail. "Well, what are you waiting for?"

"I'm not going to just dump baking soda into my machine," he protested.

"Do you want to get home or don't you?" Ivy asked.

"Of course I want to get home, but that last time was an accident. I need to consider how to control it." Angus thought for a moment. "I think I can build a compartment within the Incinerator that will release the powder in tiny increments whenever the trigger is pushed." He pulled several tools out of his belt and began working on the machine as he talked. "By elongating this here and adjusting this here ... I can tighten this. Okay, just a bit of powder, a little more. Close it up. There!"

He looked brightly at Ivy. "Here goes nothing!" He pointed the machine at the pile of vegetables. Ivy squawked with fear and dove behind the sacks. She peered out. Angus stood blinking at the rotten cabbages.

"Didn't work?" asked Ivy.

"Nope," said Angus.

"Okay. Was there anything else? After you spilled the baking soda, did anything else happen?" probed Ivy.

Angus leaned against the tower of baking soda. He was rapidly losing confidence. "Ivy, what's the use? I may as well just get used to the idea that I'm going to live on a ship the rest of my life."

"Well, I'm not! We're going to figure this out and leave this world!" The seagull clenched her wings against her sides with conviction. "Now, what else happened that day?"

Angus sighed and closed his eyes. He dug into the back of his brain trying to remember. The day he traveled to this world passed through his mind like a movie. There he was at school. Ms. Evergood at the board. He shuddered, thinking of Marge. Escaped hamster. Bus ride home. Mom at the sink. Lab. Cedar cones. Broken Incinerator. Baking soda. That was it. There was nothing else.

He opened his eyes and twirled his screwdriver around his neck. "That's it, Ivy. There's nothing ..." He stopped in the middle of a twirl and held up the screwdriver. His eyes sparkled. "Except for my screwdriver. I dropped it under the lab table."

"I can't imagine that would make a difference," said Ivy.

"And when I picked it up, I hit my head, and bit my tongue." Angus rested his hand against his lips.

"So?" asked Ivy.

"So I put my finger in my mouth. It was wet ... and then I shocked myself on the Incinerator," finished Angus.

"Moisture. We haven't tried that yet. Do you think you need that for the baking soda to work?" asked Ivy.

"I don't know. I didn't need moisture to transport the cedar cones," he said.

"True," said Ivy. "But that was before you dropped the Incinerator. Did you ever point it at yourself before you dropped it?"

"Why on earth would I do that? I thought it was burning up the cones, not transporting them. I certainly didn't want to scorch myself!" said Angus.

"Oh, yeah. Right," thought Ivy. "Maybe it's time to change the name of your machine. Seeing as it doesn't incinerate insects."

Angus bit his lip and thought a moment. "How about the Interdimensional Travel Device?"

Ivy shook her head. "Too long and sciency sounding."

"The Cross World Movement Machine?" proposed Angus.

Ivy giggled. "Movement. Sounds like you're transporting poop from one world to another. Like bowel movement. Get it?"

Angus stared at Ivy, thought for a moment, and burst out laughing. "Cross World Movement Machine! Hilarious!"

"Dimensional Doody Device!" chortled Ivy.

"The Poop Scooter!" guffawed Angus, tears rolling down his cheeks.

Angus and Ivy howled with laughter until they'd exhausted all their potty jokes.

"Okay, seriously though," gasped Angus wiping his eyes. "How about the World Jumper?"

The seagull took a deep breath to still her giggles and then considered this latest suggestion. She nodded her head. "I like it. It sounds like what I do, body jumping. But you jump whole worlds. It's a good name."

"So, let's assume my World Jumper needs water to work. How do I get it a little wet without ruining the components?" Angus looked at Ivy.

"My specialty is potions. I don't do electronics," she said.

Angus was staring at the palm of his hand. "I've got it!" he exclaimed. Ivy looked at him blankly. "Ivy, think back to when you were a human. I don't know if it's the same with girls, but when I get scared or nervous, my hands start sweating like crazy. Look, even now, my palm is a little damp. If I can reconfigure the palm grip of the World Jumper, it can use the moisture from my hand and the little puff of sodium bicarbonate to create the charge! Follow me!"

Angus clutched his World Jumper and ran recklessly from the brightly-lit hold. He didn't wait for his eyes to adjust to the dim bunkroom, and so he did not see the bucket of water left unattended by the sailor who had been washing the floor. Angus raced along, tripped over the bucket, and sailed through the air. The water spilled all over the floor. Angus involuntarily squeezed the trigger as he landed in the middle of the puddle. There was a flash and Angus sat stunned on the floor rubbing his head.

Ivy had watched it all from the hold. She strutted out of the room, toward the dazed boy. "That was a nasty fall. Are you all right, Angus?"

"Sink me! A talkin' bird! Wonder what ye're worth." He laughed and reached for her. As his hands wrapped around her flapping wings, she noticed the holes pierced into his earlobes.

"Oh great. Welcome back, BP." She poked his forehead hard with her bill. He cried out and released her to grab his head. She flew rapidly up the stairs.

Now she was going to have to search for Angus all over again.

23

The Next World

Cold pricked his ears. Cold numbed his nose and
cheeks. Cold tweeked his fingers and the tips of his
toes. He shivered and opened his eyes. He was
surrounded by snow. He felt the wet soak into his
blue jeans and his shirt. In fact, he was lying face
down in the snow.

Angus rolled over and looked around. White crystal powder as far as the eye could see. Evergreen trees in the distance drooped under its weight. The sky above shone radiant and blue.

"I'm not on a pirate ship anymore," he said aloud.

He looked frantically about him and exhaled a sigh of relief when he realized his World Jumper lay in the snow beside him. He stuffed it into the top of his pants and shivered as the cold plastic and metal touched his skin.

"Ivy? Ivy! Are you there? Ivy!" he called, looking about him. He heard nothing. No birds, no human voices, not even the sound of wind reached his ears. It appeared he was totally alone in this beautiful wintery world. At least for now.

He stood, wrapped his arms about his body, and shivered. First, he'd find some shelter and a way to stay warm. Then, he'd figure out where he was and what to do next. He smiled. He was looking forward to his next adventure. He was ready to invent.

Angus' Pirate/English Dictionary

Aft (adv.) toward the stern of a ship
Bilge rat (n.) a rat living in the bilge of a ship; an insulting name
Blimey! (colloq.) Wow!
Booty (n.) stolen goods or treasure
Bow (n.) the front of the ship
Bring a spring upon her cable (v.) come around in a different direction
Case shot (n.) a collection of small items put in cases to fire from a cannon
Davy Jones' locker (n.) the bottom of the ocean; death
Fire in the hole! (colloq.) The cannon is lit!
Head (n.) the bathroom on a ship
Hearties (n.) friends
Hold (n.) the storage room on a ship
Hornswaggle (v.) cheat someone
Jolly Roger (n.) a pirate flag with a skull and crossbones

Keelhaul (v.) punish by dragging someone under a ship, across the keel

Knave (n.) a naughty, mischievous person

Landlubber (n.) a person who lives on land; one who is clumsy at sea

Loot (n.) stolen goods, treasure

Mate, matey (n.) friend, buddy

No prey, no pay. (colloq.) If you don't work, you don't get paid.

Plunder (v.) steal; (n.) stolen goods

Port (n.) the left side of the ship when facing the bow

Powder monkey (n.) the young sailor responsible for cleaning, maintaining, and loading the cannons

Run a rig on (v.) play a trick on

Run a shot (v.) fire a cannon at

Sail ho! (colloq.) I see a ship!

Scallywag (n.) a naughty, mischievous person

Scurvy dog (n.) a disease caused by deficiency of Vitamin C; an insulting name

Shiver me timbers! (colloq.) I don't believe it!

Squiffy (adj.) severely confused

Starboard (n.) the right side of the ship when facing the bow

Stern (n.) the back of the ship

Stinkpot (n.) small clay pot filled with sulfur, rotting vegetables, or fish

Swab (v.) mop

Walk the plank (v.) be forced off the ship as a punishment

Ye (pron.) you

Ye savvy? (colloq.) Do you understand?

Ye've got me marker.   (colloq.) Thanks, I owe you
one.

Acknowledgments

In the book of life, we accomplish very little alone. At least that's been my experience. *The Pirate's Booty* would never have come to fruition without my own wonderful cast of characters. Thank you Leslie for helping me beat punctuation into submission. Jenn, only someone who really loves Angus would spend so many hours painting tiny feet. Thank you Mom and Dad for your sacrifices for and faith in me all these years. Matt, you have cheered for me since day one. Thank you to my first fans, my family and friends, for reading my scribblings. And most of all, thank you Aidan for your fierce and unflagging enthusiasm for "our book". I hope I got rid of all the boring parts now.

CPSIA information can be obtained
at www.ICGtesting.com
Printed in the USA
FSHW010115180219
55738FS